B'ELANNA TORRES WATCHED WITH HORROR AND ANGER . . .

. . . as the attack unfolded above her. The three round silver ships fired as one, launching a devastating barrage of what looked like photon torpedoes and bolts of electromagnetic energy. Above her, *Voyager* shook noticeably as first one, then another, then another blast hit. Flames shot out of a hole that suddenly appeared in the hull.

A low moan escaped her. "Run!" she cried. "Get out of here."

As if in response, *Voyager* started to turn. The nacelles began to power up for warp acceleration, then abruptly failed. On impulse power alone, *Voyager* limped off toward the red giant.

The three ships turned in pursuit. The lead ship fired again. . . .

Look for STAR TREK Fiction from Pocket Books

STAR TREK VOYAGER™

INCIDENT AT ARBUK

JOHN GREGORY BETANCOURT

POCKET BOOKS

New York   London   Toronto   Sydney   Tokyo   Singapore

This book is a work of fiction. Names, characters, places and incidents are products of the author's imagination or are used fictitiously. Any resemblance to actual events or locales or persons, living or dead, is entirely coincidental.

An *Original* Publication of POCKET BOOKS

POCKET BOOKS, a division of Simon & Schuster Inc.
1230 Avenue of the Americas, New York, NY 10020

Copyright © 1995 by Paramount Pictures. All Rights Reserved.

STAR TREK is a Registered Trademark of Paramount Pictures.

A VIACOM COMPANY

This book is published by Pocket Books, a division of Simon & Schuster Inc., under exclusive license from Paramount Pictures.

ISBN: 0-671-52048-2

First Pocket Books printing November 1995

10 9 8 7 6 5 4 3 2 1

POCKET and colophon are registered trademarks of Simon & Schuster Inc.

Printed in the U.S.A.

*This one is for my wonderful wife, Kim,
who helped immensely during its writing,
and for our new son, Ian, who didn't
(but he's cute, so we forgive him).*

*And also for John Ordover,
one of the best editors I've worked with.*

INCIDENT AT ARBUK

CHAPTER 1

Captain's Log, Stardate 48135.6

We are proceeding toward Federation space, continuing our survey of the Delta Quadrant. We have encountered few class-M planets in this sector, and fewer still sentient races. Food supplies, always a critical concern, are running low; we may have to divert power to the replicators soon if hydroponics yields continue at their present low level. Crew morale remains high, thanks to the constant efforts of Mr. Neelix, and I remain hopeful of our eventual return home.

ENSIGN HARRY KIM FROWNED DOWN AT THE COMMUNI-cations console. Something odd was going on here, he thought. Was that low-band flutter a signal? He leaned forward to study the flickering digital readouts more carefully and felt his heart beginning to pound. Then the static seemed to clear for a second and he heard what might have been frantic words in an alien language. Or was it his imagination? He couldn't quite seem to lock down the frequency. . . .

"Is something wrong, Ensign?" Captain Janeway asked him.

Harry glanced up, found himself the sole object of the captain's attention, swallowed, and felt himself blush. Her piercing blue eyes held more than casual interest; it was as if she were seeing into his thoughts and knew he'd found something interesting. In short, the captain could read him like one of her holonovels. He'd better learn to mask his excitement better, he thought.

He wished for a second that he could be as blasé about encounters with new cultures and civilizations as Tom Paris and the other bridge officers, but he couldn't help himself. He hadn't done this as often as they had—hadn't done it at all before his first mission on the *Voyager*—and every time they came upon something or someone new, it was a true first contact, one for the record books back home.

"No, Captain," he said quickly, running a hand through his short black hair to buy more time. "Uh—yes, I mean, maybe. I'm picking up what looks like a signal from the binary star system ahead."

"What kind of signal?" She tilted her head a little to the side, regarding him with interest.

"It's hard to tell with all this static. It may just be random noise caused by some natural phenomenon." There, he thought, that should cover all my bases. He met her gaze, waiting for orders.

"But you don't think so," Captain Janeway prompted.

"No, Captain," he said. *Like a holonovel.* How did she do it? He swallowed again. "I caught what I thought were frantic words a moment ago. It may be a distress signal."

She nodded curtly. "Get it cleaned up enough to understand, Ensign. I want to know what it says." She turned to the others on the bridge. "Mr. Tuvok, get me a complete readout on that system. Mr. Paris, alter course, warp three. I want a closer look."

"Yes, Captain," Tom said from the navigator's station.

Harry watched his friend lock in the coordinates, then forced his own attention back to the communications console. The readouts still fluttered a bit, sending more flickers through the green and amber lights. Quickly he locked it down. *Pay attention,* he mentally reprimanded himself. The captain expected results, and he intended to give them to her. If he'd learned anything from his months aboard *Voyager,* it was that a hundred and ten percent effort got the job done to Janeway's satisfaction—and she would have preferred a hundred and twenty percent.

First things first, though. Harry began to filter out all the high-band emissions. One of his instructors at Starfleet Academy, Dr. Dorian Schweitzer, had once compared honing in on a distant signal to creating a sculpture from a block of marble. "The trick," Dr. Schweitzer had said, strutting up and down before the podium in his gray one-piece suit with his arms behind his back, tossing his shock of white hair this way and that as he raked his sea green eyes over the class, "is in viewing a clouded signal as a buried

3

structure. Like the sculptor who chips away everything from a block of marble *except* his statue; you must eliminate every signal except the one you're looking for."

At the time Harry had thought it a far-fetched analogy, but over the months on *Voyager* he'd come to see the truth of it. This distress call, for example, fit Dr. Schweitzer's example. He knew the signal existed; he merely had to uncover it.

He began to slide down the frequency range, eliminating one noise source after another. Still static buzzed in his ear. Biting his lip in frustration, he continued to work.

"I have that report, Captain," Tuvok said in his low, even voice from the security station.

"Let's hear it," Janeway said.

"We are approaching a binary star system composed of a red giant orbited by a white dwarf. There are no planets, no asteroids, and little in the way of cosmic debris. The gravitational pulls of both stars, coupled with their strong gravimetric fields, virtually prohibit any orbiting bodies. Logically, the signal must therefore originate from a ship or a starbase of some sort. If Mr. Kim is correct and there is a signal, of course."

Harry, half listening, felt his ears begin to burn. There was a signal, he told himself. He'd heard it.

He shot a quick glance at Mr. Tuvok, but the Vulcan's dark-skinned face was turned away. Was he being sarcastic? Were Vulcans *ever* sarcastic? Harry didn't think he'd ever know the answer to either question. As much as Harry's grandmother had insisted the gateway to the soul lay through the eyes,

Harry had never been able to read anything in Tuvok's eyes.

Sarcasm or not, he had a job to do, and staring at Tuvok's back wasn't going to help. The Vulcan, arms braced against the console as he leaned forward to examine the readout with a perfectionist's attention to detail, looked like he'd be there for the next half hour.

I'll show him, Harry thought suddenly. He quickly locked out two more nearby quasars, which had been spitting radio waves like Morse code, and continued through the process of eliminating all the outside noise. *It's just like they taught at Starfleet Academy,* he thought. *This exercise could have been out of one of Dr. Schweitzer's communications texts.*

Suddenly a flickering, ghostlike image appeared on his monitor. Harry found himself staring into the face of an alien the like of which he'd never seen before. What looked like writhing gray tentacles covered the top of its elongated head. It had a small, round mouth, but no eyes, ears, or nose that he could see— in fact, no apparent external sensory organs of any kind. But it proved him right, he thought with a touch of satisfaction. The alien was gesturing wildly with its arms, and he could see its mouth moving, but had no sound as yet.

And then the picture vanished again, lost in a burst of static. They were just too far away, he thought with a twinge of disappointment. He'd have to try something else to get through.

He had one last trick. Instead of using the ship's communications arrays to pick up the signal, he manually routed the pickup through the ship's internal wiring. *Voyager* might be the most advanced ship in the fleet, with all kinds of bioelectric couplings, but it still had more than its share of old-fashioned wires. He'd once overheard Dr. Schweitzer bragging about successfully picking up a faint Romulan signal by using his whole ship as a receiver. But would it work for him?

His long fingers danced across the controls, rerouting the communications arrays to auxiliary channels. He couldn't just shut them off, he thought, in case an important message came through. Then, keeping his attention tightly focused on the main readouts, he experimented with channeling signal feeds from subsystems. It wasn't in any of the official manuals, but he thought it just might work.

The moment he finished rerouting the pickup, interstellar static roared over the channel. Wincing, he lowered the volume. So much for the music of the spheres, he thought. Now that he no longer had the automatic fine-tuning abilities of the communications arrays at his command, he would have to manually filter out all the low-band noise.

He started by once again locking out the two quasars' signals, and the moment he did, he heard another burst of frantic-sounding words, this time accompanied by a flickery image. He sighed with relief. He hadn't made a fool out of himself. Then he grinned; B'Elanna and Chakotay weren't the only ones with tricks up their sleeves.

He continued the filtration process and was rewarded when he finally got a firm lock on the picture. From the alien's frantic gestures and words, he figured it had to be a distress call. He'd been right on that one, too. He nodded slowly to himself, did a little more fine-tuning, then looked at Captain Janeway.

"Captain," he announced. "I have a low-level audio and video signal."

"On the front screen when you're ready, Mr. Kim." The captain looked up and tapped her comm link. "Neelix, report to the bridge, please."

Harry routed the signal to the large viewscreen at the front of the bridge. On such a large monitor the image's poor quality seemed a hundred times worse. White static crawled across the picture, and frames dropped out every second or two. Maybe he could do a little more fine-tuning. He tried adjusting the stabilizers, but even with the computer helping to compensate and with *Voyager* drawing steadily nearer to the broadcast source, the picture stubbornly refused to improve.

Harry realized he'd been holding his breath and forced himself to exhale. The picture wasn't going to get any clearer. He glanced around the bridge. The rest of the crew seemed just as spellbound, he thought, even Tom and Chakotay. Perhaps they weren't as blasé about first contacts after all.

"I'm afraid I can't get a better lock on the signal," he said half-apologetically.

"Considering the type and strength of the signal," Tuvok said dryly, "you should not be picking it up at all. Your work is above reproach, Ensign."

"Agreed, well done, Mr. Kim," Captain Janeway said, glancing back at him. "Now it's time for another miracle. Can we send a message back to the alien?"

"We can try," Harry said, "but I don't think there's any chance of it receiving our transmission. Its equipment is nowhere near as sophisticated or as powerful as *Voyager's*."

The alien continued its frantic speech, still gesticulating wildly. Its language was glottal but articulated, full of weird grunts and whistles. It sounded afraid, Harry thought, and when it raised two quivering hands in what might have been a gesture of supplication, he thought it seemed somehow desperate.

"What are our chances of a translation?" Captain Janeway asked.

"None yet," Harry said. "The computer has been unable to identify any of what it's saying."

"Your analysis, Mr. Tuvok?" she asked, turning to look at him.

"He would appear to be in some distress," the Vulcan said. "There is nothing noticeably wrong with his craft that I can see from this transmission, but without any real familiarity with its design, I cannot be certain I would notice if something had malfunctioned. Caution would seem to be indicated, however. If his craft is caught in a gravimetric tide of some sort, we do not want to suffer the same fate."

"Noted, Mr. Tuvok," Captain Janeway said. "However, I will not ignore a distress call."

"I did not recommend ignoring it," Tuvok said evenly. "I merely recommended caution as we approach."

Harry's gaze drifted beyond the alien to the interior of its small spaceship. Gleaming silver globes—controls of some sort, he assumed—covered one whole wall; another held a large round viewport that faced out upon stars and the red giant that made up half of this star system. The red giant wasn't a true red in color, he noticed. Yellows and oranges and browns mottled its surface, surging in flares, deepening in sunspots.

He blinked. The red giant was growing steadily larger, he realized. The alien's ship seemed to be spinning lazily, as if it were out of control.

"Captain—" he began.

"I see it, Mr. Kim," she said. "He does indeed appear to be drifting. Maximum speed, Mr. Paris. Get me an estimated time of arrival."

"Aye, Captain," Tom said.

Harry felt the almost undetectable distant thrum of the engines deepen through the soles of his feet as Tom increased their warp. He only hoped they'd be in time to help.

Tom continued, "One hour and fifty-three minutes until we enter the system. One hour and fifty-nine minutes until we reach his present position. His ship will have drifted behind the white dwarf by the time we arrive, however."

"Open hailing frequencies," Captain Janeway said. "We'll try a message."

"Aye, Captain," Harry said, complying.

Janeway stepped forward to face the viewscreen. Her back grew even straighter as she drew herself up to her full height, and Harry heard the crack of authority in her voice when she spoke: "This is Captain Kathryn Janeway of the Federation Starship *Voyager*. We are responding to your call. Is your ship in trouble? Is there anything we can do to assist you?"

The alien continued to jabber frantically. If it heard

her, it made no sign. *It didn't*, Harry thought suddenly. *There's no way it could have picked up our message.* He found he'd been hoping that some fluke, some trick of subspace like the one that had first brought the distress call to him, would in return bring their message to the alien. But that had been too much to expect.

Then a jolt of surprise shot through him. What was *that?*

Slowly, through the little ship's viewport, another vessel had begun to come into view. He saw one large group of misshapen silver globules connected by tiny gray tubes, then another, then another. It looked like an old-fashioned model of a molecule, he thought, only without a molecule's grace and structure. This ship seemed to be a haphazard jumble of chambers, one linked to another with no sense of design or purpose that he could discern.

Then he realized the silver globules weren't malformed, but melted. Some great blast of energy had half turned them to slag.

Harry felt his heart begin to pound again. *It's been through a battle*, he thought. *We're heading right into a war zone.*

The alien glanced out its viewport, saw the damaged vessel, whistled frantically—and then the picture cut out. White static hissed and spat across the screen. Harry quickly put up a forward view of the two stars in the binary system.

"What happened?" Captain Janeway demanded.

"It stopped transmitting," he said.

She paused a second, frowning, then tapped her comm link again. "Neelix to the bridge!" she said.

* * *

When the ship's intercom chirped and Captain Janeway said "Neelix to the bridge!" for the second time, Neelix sighed, wiped his hands on his food-spattered yellow-and-pink checked apron, and tapped his own badge, which he had pinned to his bright orange-and-purple striped shirt.

"I'm quite busy with lunch preparations, Captain," he said. "Can it wait?" That woman needed to learn patience, he thought. It was the one virtue she seemed to lack.

"Not this time," she said.

"Then I'm on my way."

Sighing, he turned to survey the ship's galley. Pots containing bright blue, green, and pink liquids bubbled, steamed, or stewed, letting off the most delicious aromas. He had spent the last two hours rushing from one cooking vessel to the next, first stirring, then seasoning, then tasting, then stirring again, but all that might be wasted now. The captain didn't seem to care about the vast efforts he expended on her behalf to prepare the crew's meals. In fact, as far as he could tell, everyone aboard—Federation and Maquis alike—placed little or no real value on his time and sweat.

He blamed replicators. Instant food—feh, what an insult to the sensitive palate. Sometimes he thought the crew actually *preferred* synthetics to his gourmet creations.

Still, perhaps he could save lunch. He needed an assistant, someone who could look after things for a few minutes. Normally he would have asked Kes, but she was busy studying Federation medical texts with the holographic doctor and he knew how important that was to her. But maybe he could find someone else.

Fortunately Paul Fairman happened to be standing behind him. The ensign was a tall blond man with a short beard who had been part of the Maquis ship's crew before their integration with *Voyager*'s. Fairman didn't seem particularly busy; in fact, if anything he was being a nuisance.

"I need you to stir the pots until I get back," Neelix said, suddenly making up his mind and thrusting a large wooden spoon into Fairman's hand.

"Me?" Fairman protested, trying to hand it back. "Oh, no! Absolutely not! I came here to ask a favor, not get drafted into kitchen duty!"

Neelix sighed. Despite all their technological advances, humans just didn't understand the way the galaxy worked. Fairman was a typical example.

"Let me explain the barter process," he said, trying to keep it slow and simple. Fairman had been following him through the galley for the last half hour, badgering him to scrounge up a portable external power supply—something small that could be used in the privacy of his cabin. "You do something for me," Neelix said, "then in exchange I do something for you. It's a basic trade of goods and services. Surely humans grasp it."

"It's a matter of unsuitability in my case," Fairman protested. "As everyone on board knows, you are a master chef; I have never been this near a stove before in my life."

"I know, I know," Neelix said, letting a bit of Fairman's whine echo in his own voice, "you're just a poor mercenary who hired on with the Maquis to fight

Cardassians and got sucked out to the Delta Quadrant against your will. But you eat the same as everyone else on board, and that means you can pitch in here for a few minutes."

"But I *know* I'll do something wrong and ruin your preparations."

"I'll take the risk!" Neelix said. "Stir the pots for me until I get back, and I'll look into finding you that power supply!"

Fairman brightened. "You will?"

"Just . . . stir!" Neelix blamed his reputation: he'd always said he could get anything for anybody, and what did he ask in return? Nothing but a little respect. Well, it was time to collect.

"I'll try." Fairman took a deep breath and regarded the spoon as if it were some poisonous insect that had crawled from the woodwork. "What do I do first?"

Neelix began pointing to pots. "Make sure that one doesn't boil over, that one doesn't burn, and *above all keep stirring!*" He pushed the spoon's bowl-end into a steaming pot of finely chopped yellow *phu* and made a circular motion with one finger. Humans could be absolutely *clueless* at times, he thought with near despair.

Slowly, his distaste for the chore obvious, Fairman began to stir the pot.

"That's it!" Neelix cried. He ran for the doors, shouting over his shoulder, "I'll be back as soon as I can!"

He bounded up the gently curving corridor. What could the captain possibly want from him this time, he wondered. Whatever it was, he'd get it for her. As always, it would be Neelix to the rescue. He had a reputation to protect, after all.

He entered the turbolift. "Bridge," he said, and it whisked him up toward his destination. How Janeway and the Federation ever managed to get so far without him, he didn't know. . . .

CHAPTER 2

"Mr. Neelix," Captain Janeway said a bit sternly when the little alien strolled onto the bridge. She had to be careful in her choice of words, she knew; she needed Neelix and Kes a lot more than they needed *Voyager*, and Neelix in particular seemed to have an all too fragile ego. "As part of this ship's crew," she said, "I would appreciate it if you put top priority on my orders."

"Of course, Captain," he said. "As you know, I've always placed your needs highest on my list of priorities."

"That's not quite what I meant," Janeway began. Then she gave a mental sigh: Neelix just didn't think the way humans did, and he wasn't going to change no matter what she said. He was staring at her with wide, innocent eyes. How could she reprimand him for not understanding the way things worked on a Federation starship? She was having enough trouble getting the Maquis to bend to Federation rules.

"Never mind," she said. She gave a a nod to the forward monitor, which now showed a close-up of the binary star system they were approaching, the fiery red giant orbited by a white dwarf. "Do you know anything about this system?"

Neelix squinted up at the viewscreen and seemed to search his memory. "The big red star looks familiar," he said after a long moment. Janeway felt a surge of hope. "Ah, yes, now I recognize it—the Arbuk system, of course." He waved a hand dismissively at it. "There's nothing there, Captain. Nothing of interest, anyway—no planets, no food, no resources of any kind. Best to steer clear of it. If I remember my charts correctly, I believe there are some pretty strong gravimetric currents around that white dwarf."

"Thank you," Janeway said.

"Is that all?" he asked.

"One more thing." She turned and nodded to Harry Kim, who began a playback of the alien's transmission. As Neelix watched, Janeway tried to gauge his reaction. She thought she saw puzzlement. When he began nodding, she knew he recognized the alien's species. Perhaps he'd be able to shed some light on what was going on after all.

"What can you tell us?" she asked him.

"It's just a Sperian," he said with a dismissive wave, "nothing to be concerned about."

"It appears to be a distress call," she said. "I think that's cause for concern."

"The Sperians are always very animated talkers.

It's one of their many, many, *many* annoying traits, and I strongly suggest leaving them and this system strictly alone."

"Do you understand their language?"

"Not a word." From the way he puffed out his chest, he seemed almost proud of the fact, Janeway thought. It was as though he took great personal satisfaction from his ignorance, which seemed quite unlike him. There had to be more going on here than she saw on the surface.

"But you've dealt with them," she prompted.

"Unfortunately, yes. The few dealings I've had with them have all been through middlemen. Now, if you'd asked me about the Cyclets of Mernical Three or the Bandacians of Ordinia Nine, well, I could provide you with any manner of details—"

Janeway, feeling her patience beginning to fray, cut him off with a curt wave. "Yes, but I need to know about Sperians now. Is there anything else you can tell me? Anything at all helpful in dealing with them?"

"Such as . . . ?" Neelix asked.

Was he being deliberately obtuse? If so, two could play at that game, Janeway thought. If he wanted her to drag the information out of him bit by bit, she'd do it.

"Well," she said slowly, "are they involved in any wars or long-standing conflicts which might suddenly have erupted into violence?"

"The Sperians?" Neelix threw back his head and laughed. "In two words, *im*-possible. Everyone in this quadrant avoids them, and with good reason. You can waste days arguing with a Sperian over trivialities. The last time I dealt with one—and this was through a middleman, mind you—it took me an extra three weeks to buy a cargo of dabinroot simply because the Sperian argued over every detail of the transaction from start to finish, whether it was in his best interests or not. It annoyed him no end when I finally gave in on every point just to get on with my trip."

"So they're argumentative," she mused.

"No," he said, "they are beyond argumentative. They have raised haggling to a fine art. It has become so ingrained in their culture and in their psyche that they *have* to argue. Not even the Kazon bother them. It's simply not worth the effort. And if someone were foolish enough to actually conquer them—my mind boggles at the thought of the bureaucracy that would spring up to even *attempt* to assimilate their society."

Neelix leaned forward and dropped his voice to an almost conspiratorial whisper. Janeway found herself leaning forward, too, and had to force herself to stop. Neelix had an almost infectious influence on all of those around him, she thought.

"*That*," Neelix said, "is why I refuse to deal with Sperians unless it can't possibly be avoided. I get into quite enough pointless arguments already, thank you, without Sperians."

"That's very interesting," Janeway said. "Thank you, Mr. Neelix. As always, your advice has been invaluable."

He shook his head sadly. "But you're not going to take it," he said almost accusingly.

"I'm afraid I can't pass by a distress call, no matter who it's from."

"You'll be sorry."

"Quite possibly," she admitted.

"Is that all?"

"I'll let you know if we need anything further."

Neelix threw up his hands in seeming despair and hurried back toward the turbolift. "She called me up here just to ask about an empty system and Sperians," Janeway heard him muttering. "Sperians! If lunch is ruined . . ."

The doors closed around him. Janeway took a deep, cleansing breath and noticed Chakotay trying to hide a smile. Infectious indeed, she thought. Sometimes you needed to laugh to break the tension, but this didn't strike her as one of those times. From the look of things, that Sperian was in serious trouble.

"Did I miss something amusing?" she asked her first officer.

"He *is* quite a character," Chakotay observed. He covered his mouth with his left hand, trying to hide his expression with a look of serious concern.

Janeway decided to let it pass. She glanced back at the communications station. "Any luck in reestablishing contact with the Sperian, Ensign?" she asked Harry Kim.

"No, Captain," he said. "I'm still trying, but I'm not getting anything."

"Keep at it," she said. She turned to Chakotay. "You have the bridge, Commander. I'll be in my ready room. Call me if there's any change."

"Aye, Captain," he said.

Two hours to kill, she thought. *Time to try to catch up on my paperwork. And maybe a soothing cup of coffee. . . .*

* * *

Fifteen minutes wasn't long, Neelix thought optimistically as he rushed back toward the galley. He called cheerful greetings to the half-dozen crewmen he passed, and they nodded back. How much damage could one human have done to lunch in just fifteen minutes? All Fairman had to do was stir a few pots, after all. It was so simple a spindle-kitten could have done it with five paws tied behind its metathorax.

As he neared the galley, however, a feeling of supreme dread came over him. For a second he couldn't figure out what was wrong. Then he smelled the faint, unpleasant odor of burning *paga* stew.

"No!" he cried.

He ran the last few steps to the galley doors. When they whisked open to admit him, a thick, greasy cloud of black smoke rolled out. He reeled back, trying to fan it away with his hands. *I was only gone fifteen minutes,* he thought numbly. *It can't possibly be as bad as it looks—can it?*

Coughing, trying not to breathe, he dashed forward into the heart of the conflagration. His eyes began to burn and tear, but there was nothing he could do about it. At least the automatic fire extinguishers hadn't gone off this time, he thought. He still remembered battling a flood of fire-retardant foam the day he'd tried to set up a barbecue pit.

Fairman, clutching a wet cloth over his mouth and nose, stood at the heart of the disaster. He was waving his wooden spoon helplessly over the clouds of dense black smoke roiling up around the pot of *paga* stew. He hadn't stirred it enough, Neelix realized, and the pot had boiled over onto the heating element. That's where the smoke was actually coming from.

Grabbing the thermal mittens he used for moving hot pans and utensils, he lifted the stew onto a nearby counter, where he knew it would be safe. At least Fairman had had the sense to turn off the heating element, he thought. The smoke was just the after-effect of the spill, not an ongoing problem. It was, as he'd once heard Tom Paris so succinctly put it, all smoke and no fire.

He shouldered Fairman out of the way, lifted the heating element out of its setting, carried it across the kitchen, and dropped in into the tub of water he'd used to soak plates and silverware clean. Steam hissed around the metal coils for a few seconds, then slowly subsided.

"Why didn't you stir it?" Neelix demanded.

Dropping his spoon, choking and gasping for air, Fairman staggered away from the kitchen area and toward the doors. His face had turned a pasty gray-green color, and black soot smudged the tip of his nose.

"Go see the doctor," Neelix called after him. "There may be aftereffects if you breathed in too much smoke. And try to take it easy for the rest of the afternoon!"

He couldn't tell if Fairman had heard him or not. Well, he'd worry about it later. First things first, after all, and that meant getting lunch back on schedule. The early shift would be here in less than an hour. As the ship's self-appointed morale officer as well as chef, he couldn't disappoint them. He could only imagine the looks on their faces if they found burnt food and a room full of noxious smoke waiting instead of a delicious hot meal.

He hurried to the back wall and the room's environmental-control system. "Computer," he said, "increase air filtration to maximum."

A soft sequence of beeps answered. "Acknowledged," the computer said. "Air vents open."

A wave of cool, fresh air swept over him. He'd let the ship's filtration system do the hard work of removing the smoke, he thought with a measure of satisfaction. There were a few advantages in being aboard a ship as advanced as the *Voyager*, after all.

Suddenly an alarm began to sound, and he jumped in surprise, looking around in all directions. What now? It didn't seem to be a red or yellow alert—

Tuvok's voice came over the galley's intercom: "One of the crew has reported a blazing fire ravaging the kitchen," the Vulcan said. "However, our internal sensors are not picking up anything beyond your usual heat sources. What is your assessment of the situation, Mr. Neelix?"

"There isn't any fire," Neelix said. "Lunch boiled over, that's all."

"Understood," the Vulcan said. The alarm stopped. "I will leave you to regain control of the situation. Tuvok out."

"Regain control of the situation," Neelix repeated with a snort. "I had it under control all along."

He returned to his collection of bubbling and simmering pots, evaluating what was left of the meal. Every dish except for the *paga* stew still simmered happily, though the Blaxan pudding had a dingy gray film on top from exposure to spoke. Quickly he skimmed the pudding, then took a quick taste. He didn't think anyone would notice a little smoke flavoring, considering its strong, delightfully pungent taste.

Lastly he checked the pot of yellow-brown stew. It smelled fine, he thought, but when he tried to dip his little finger in for a quick taste, he discovered it had congealed into a hard lump. Well, he'd just have to dump it out, carve it into slices, and declare it *paga*loaf. No sense in letting perfectly good food go to waste, especially considering how short supplies had grown on board. Besides, it might be delicious. He wouldn't know until he tried it, after all. And if it wasn't quite up to snuff, he'd try a sweetly pungent Drayonian red sauce with it.

The air had already cleared noticeably; he could see the back wall once more. In a few minutes, the galley would be back to normal. Lunch had been saved.

What would they do without me? he thought happily. He turned the pot of *paga*loaf on its side and watched the mass of gelatinous yellowish goo flecked with brown chucks of *paga* slide out. The meal would be ready right on schedule—and, as always, it had been Neelix to the rescue.

Chakotay stared intently at the two stars on the viewscreen, one red giant and one white dwarf. In all his years in Starfleet and with the Maquis he'd seen more than his share of action, and unless he was mistaken, the damage to that immense ship of linked silver globes had come from a high-powered energy weapon of some kind. He knew of no natural phenomenon that could melt durasteel plating on one part of a ship while leaving another part completely unscathed. Clearly it had been through a battle.

But why fight for a star system with no resources? He had to be missing something, he thought. Could this system be a staging ground for larger military action?

"Play back the alien's transmission," he told Harry Kim. "I want to hear it again."

As the ensign complied, Chakotay leaned forward, watching raptly. When the damaged vessel began to show through the little ship's viewport, he said, "Freeze it there."

He moved forward to examine the image. Here's where the clue would be—assuming a clue was here to be found. "Magnify." The viewport grew larger; now it filled the whole screen.

He'd never seen anything quite like the Sperians' spherical construction. It seemed strangely impractical, unless they were trying to decentralize the command structure. That kind of arrangement had worked for the Borg. But somehow he didn't think it was the case here.

If anything, the ship seemed like a series of interlocking rooms, he thought. On the sections that hadn't been blasted away or melted to slag, he spotted what appeared to be tiny round viewports. Were they on scale with the one through which he now looked? If so, that vessel had to be immense . . . or not a vessel at all. Could this be a space station? He couldn't see the whole of the structure, and without actually being there he could only guess at its true dimensions. He thought it must be huge, the size of a city.

That offered some possibilities. A space city in a deserted system would be a good place for a secret research base. If someone else had had found out and objected, it might well explain everything they had seen. If only Neelix had been able to tell them more about the Sperians.

"End it," he said to Harry, who complied quickly. The ensign had the makings of a fine officer, he thought. Just get a few more seasons under his belt so he didn't get so excited over everything they came across and he'd be fine.

Chakotay crossed to the science station, where Ensign Marta Dvorak had been running a series of analyses on the system. She was a possibility for permanent assignment to the bridge crew: B'Elanna had noticed her work in Engineering and brought it to his attention. Like B'Elanna, Ensign Dvorak dropped out of Starfleet Academy; unlike B'Elanna—and like him—she had left specifically to join the Maquis. She had been a second-year science student, near the top of her class, with a promising career ahead of her. Then her homeworld, New Russia, had been ceded to Cardassian rule in the peace treaty. Of course she'd rallied to the cause.

He sympathized with her motives, understood her background, but found her still to be something of a mystery. She kept herself deliberately distant: cool, aloof, professional. In many ways she reminded him of Tuvok. Perhaps, he mused, that was one of the things about her that intrigued him.

Dvorak looked up as he approached. "Sir?"

"What do you have on the system so far, Ensign?"

"The white dwarf is spitting a lot of radio and

electromagnetic static bursts, which would be perfect camouflage for anything going on here."

"What do you suspect?"

"I have no evidence to support any theory."

"Never mind, please speculate."

"This would seem an ideal place to conduct secret experiments or research, sir. Both civilian . . . and military."

Chakotay nodded slowly. A perceptive analysis. He'd known she had promise. "I had already thought of that myself. It's isolated, it's got an abundance of solar energy, and if the Sperians are as universally shunned as Neelix seemed to indicate, who would think of watching them here?"

Marta glanced over at Tom Paris. "We'll be able to take some long-range sensor scans in a few minutes, sir."

"Do so."

"Aye, sir." She turned back to her console.

Chakotay returned to the captain's chair and sat, staring up again at the red giant and white dwarf stars drawing nearer by the second. The situation bothered him. He had a distinctly uneasy feeling they were about to get mixed up in a dangerous situation.

One of the privileges of being captain of a starship, Kathryn Janeway mused in her ready room, *is having your own replicator.* "Coffee, personal setting number three," she said. A steaming mug materialized in the little wall unit before her. She took it and sipped gently: just a hint of honey and chestnuts, but it tasted so good. Later she knew she'd regret using one of her replicator rations so frivolously, but right now she needed *coffee*, and somehow nothing else would do.

Cradling the warm mug in her hands, she returned to her desk and sat. She had a thousand little tasks still to do today, from reviewing the ship's latest inventory lists to approving Neelix's proposed menu for the week, but her thoughts kept returning to the Sperian and whatever lay waiting for them in the Arbuk system. War or natural disaster? Too late to help or just in time? *If only I knew more about the situation,* she thought. *If only Neelix had been more helpful.*

Chakotay's voice interrupted: "Captain, long-range sensors are picking up heavy construction activity in the Arbuk system."

"What are they building?"

"It might be some kind of space station. We can't tell its exact purpose, but it seems to be going up quickly."

"Are they building it or repairing it?"

"Building it, Captain. This is not the same structure we saw through the Sperian's viewport."

"How long until we're in visual range?"

"Another eight minutes."

"I'll be right there."

It never rains but it pours, she thought. She smelled her coffee, closed her eyes for a second to savor the aroma, then sipped again. Delicious. *No matter how far we go,* she thought, *we never can replace the sights and smells and tastes of home.* Quickly signing off on Neelix's menu (*baba-root* stew? *matewai* over *sput?* grilled *thox?* demi-smoked *phu?*—perhaps it tasted better than it sounded), she scanned the duty roster long enough to swap two ensigns so they didn't pull double shifts, then punched up a picture of her fiancé.

"I'll be home soon," she whispered.

Suddenly the coffee didn't taste as good. She drained it, rose, and went out to see what the Arbuk system had to offer.

CHAPTER 3

TOM PARIS COULDN'T HELP BUT STUDY MARTA DVORAK from the corners of his eyes as she moved through her duties like an automaton. She had a nice face, with a strong jaw, high cheekbones, and piercing blue eyes. But he'd never seen her smile. And he'd never gotten anywhere with her when he tried to strike up a conversation . . . she'd kept herself deliberately distant, deliberately cool and professional. But then, he thought, that mood tended to dominate the ship. They hadn't had much to smile about since ending up in the Delta Quadrant. Seventy thousand light-years from home . . . it seemed an impossible journey back, and at times, late at night, alone in his cabin, he felt the isolation more keenly than he had in prison.

He took a deep, cleansing breath and forced his thoughts back to the bridge. *I've gotten my life and my commission back,* he thought. *The past is behind me now*. He'd done his time, and he'd earned his early release.

He glanced at Marta Dvorak again and allowed himself to wonder if she might enjoy a picnic. He had a couple of holodeck programs that might well pull her from her bleak-seeming mood. . . .

"Captain on the bridge," Harry Kim said.

Tom focused his attention on the controls before him. Keep it business as usual, he thought. He owed Captain Janeway everything; she'd given him his second chance. He was on top of things one hundred and ten percent whenever she was on the bridge.

He heard her sit behind him and drew himself up straighter in his seat. Anything she wanted, he'd give her.

"Any changes?" she asked Chakotay.

"Long-range scans—" Tom heard the first officer begin.

Tom allowed his eyes to drift ever so slightly toward Ensign Dvorak once more. One hundred and five percent today, he thought. Beautiful women had always been a weakness. And Marta was very beautiful.

He licked his lips. A holodeck picnic might be what she needed . . . and what he needed, too.

Kathryn Janeway nodded as she listened to Chakotay's report: nothing that hadn't already occurred to her, she thought, right down to his theory about the space city. She and Chakotay seemed to be operating more and more on the same wavelength. At times it was a blessing, but when you needed new insights it could be a curse. They wouldn't know the full story until they reached the Sperian who had sent out the distress call.

Her attention turned to the bridge crew. Harry Kim had been watching Tom who had been watching Ensign Dvorak when she came out of her ready room. All three looked spit-and-polish ready for inspection: uniforms regulation, hair neat, at their stations. But, as she settled back into her chair, she couldn't help but reflect on the subtle changes in bridge dynamics going on around her. A good captain was supposed to spot things like this, she thought. It was an old-fashioned domino effect: Tom had become a role model for Harry Kim, and when he began to drift from the hard line of duty, Harry usually followed.

She knew why Tom was drifting, too. She'd discovered months before that Tom tended to channel his impatience and stir-crazy impulses into an overactive social life. When it started to intrude onto the bridge, it meant the time had come for her to find shore-leave facilities for the whole crew. Keeping her people healthy both mentally and physically had always been a top priority, and here in the Delta Quadrant, so far from any starbase or proper recreational facilities, it became doubly important. After they finished with their rescue mission—if rescue mission it was—she'd have Neelix recommend a quiet planet where everyone could enjoy a little well-deserved R&R.

"I want a long-range view of the system," she said.

Harry punched it up. The red giant appeared before them, its distant fiery surface a ruby blur mottled with darker patches that had to be sunspots and brighter orange and yellow areas that had to be solar flares. To the left, made as tiny as insects by the vast distance, a swarm of round silver starships moved like bees around a metal framework. They seemed hard at work, either building something or taking it down. *Taking it down. That's something that didn't occur to Chakotay,* she thought.

"Tuvok?"

"This doesn't look like a war zone," she said slowly.

"No sign of fighting or damage of any kind," he said, "unless it has already been repaired. This would appear to be a normal industrial scene."

"We are now entering the Arbuk system," Tom Paris said.

"Drop speed to warp two," Janeway said. "We don't want to alarm them."

"Captain," said Marta Dvorak, "I'm picking up no life-form readings from that construction crew."

"Is there any interference blocking your readings?"

"Partially, but I compensated for it."

"Perhaps the construction equipment is automated," Chakotay suggested.

Janeway nodded slowly. That might well account for their continued work if a battle of some kind were going on elsewhere in the system. "Keep scanning, Ensign. Let me know if anything changes."

"Yes, Captain," she said. "Another space construction is coming into view around the white dwarf."

"Drop to impulse power," Janeway ordered, leaning forward. Another construction? Could it be the damaged space station?

Tom Paris's hands caressed the controls. *Voyager* decelerated.

Slowly an immense object emerged from behind

the star. The white dwarf's corona made everything hazy and distorted at first, but it quickly took shape—half-melted tubes and spheres, all interconnected, first tens then hundreds then thousands of them, and more kept appearing as they rounded the star.

How big is it? she wondered, feeling a little awed as more and more of the station kept coming into view. It had to cover several cubic kilometers, she realized. She had only seen a tiny portion of it through the Sperian's viewport. It wasn't so much a space station as a space city, larger than anything in the Federation, larger than anything she'd ever heard of.

But the city didn't really need to occupy so much space—its construction wasted a lot of resources. But perhaps there were sociological reasons behind it, she reflected, some need to put more distance than a mere bulkhead could provide between one another. If the Sperians were as argumentative as Neelix claimed, perhaps they slept or worked in isolation to avoid such conflict.

"Reduce magnification, Ensign," she said to Harry.

"Aye, Captain," he said.

The image changed to a more distant view, showing a larger portion of the complex. It had all come into sight.

The city had been devastated. Most of one side had been outright destroyed. There was simply no other way to put it, she thought with a growing sense of unease. What kind of weapon could cause this kind of damage—vaporizing hundreds of square meters of the city and half melting most of the rest?

She found it hard to put the city into its proper

perspective; in space it was hard to measure distance or size without any real spatial references present, but judging by what she saw, it had to be even larger than she'd thought.

"This construction covers approximately two-point-six-four cubic kilometers," Tuvok said, as if reading her thoughts. "There is no sign of industrial activity of any kind, Captain."

"I'm picking up a few scattered energy readings," Marta added from her station. "It's not completely dead."

Harry Kim suddenly said, "I'm picking up the distress signal again, Captain. Its source must have been behind the white dwarf."

"On the viewscreen," she said. Perhaps they could get some answers now.

The signal switched to show the interior of the small spacecraft once more, this time in perfect clarity. The same alien stood there, the tendrils on its head slowly undulating like anemones in an Earthly ocean, but now it seemed calmer, almost resigned. When it spoke, its words filled with sharp tweets and whistles, she couldn't help but pick up on its fear.

"Hail him," she said.

"No response," Harry said.

Suddenly the picture went to static for half a second; then the alien reappeared, repeating the same twitter of words, making the same motions with its thin gray hands. The message was on a loop, she thought.

"The computer still isn't able to translate," Harry said.

"I recommend going to yellow alert, Captain,"

Tuvok said. "Based on the state of that space city, we may be heading into an armed conflict."

"Agreed," she said. An amber light began to flash. "Where precisely is that signal coming from, Mr. Kim?" She didn't think it was a trap, but she wanted to make sure.

"Somewhere beyond the space station," Harry said. "I'm having trouble pinpointing its exact location due to heavy interference from the white dwarf."

"Keep after it," she said.

"Dropping to half impulse power," Tom Paris said. "Two hundred and eighty thousand kilometers and closing."

Janeway stood and moved forward, studying the ravaged city more closely. What had happened here? A few round lights showed in the remaining intact viewports in the space city, but most remained dark. She saw no movement anywhere. Some sixth sense warned her of danger, sending little prickles of apprehension up her spine.

"Going to quarter impulse power," Tom said. "Two hundred thousand kilometers and closing."

"Is anyone alive in the city, or is it completely automated?" she asked.

"Sensors show no life signs," Marta said slowly. "However, there are bodies." She looked up, the horror of it plain of her face. "Nearly thirteen thousand bodies, Captain!"

Janeway barely managed to keep her shock from showing. A good commander was calm in all situations, she told herself, no matter how horrible.

"Double-check that," she said, but she knew inside the number had to be too low. How many more had been vaporized in the attack? A lump filled in her throat. Whole wars had been fought with fewer casualties than this.

"Confirmed, Captain. Thirteen thousand and twelve bodies."

"Cause of death?" she asked.

"Primarily explosive decompression."

"The whole space city has lost its internal atmosphere," Tuvok said. "There do not appear to be any functional self-sealing bulkheads in the remaining sections."

"Did they malfunction? Or was it sabotage?"

"Unknown, Captain."

"There's nothing we can do for this city now," she said grimly. It would take them weeks to round up all the bodies. "Perhaps we can help the survivors." Hopefully some of them managed to evacuate, she thought.

"Sensors are picking up another, even larger construction ahead," Tuvok said in a flat voice. "I must recommend red alert."

"Maintain yellow alert," she said, "but prepare to raise shields. We don't want anyone to mistake us for a hostile ship—but we don't want to get caught in a crossfire, either. Mr. Paris, steer fifty kilometers wide of that space city. Head for the next construction, one-eighth impulse power."

"Aye, Captain."

"Ensign Kim—" she began.

"On the viewscreen now," Harry said.

Janeway stared. The next Sperian complex had been built to completely different specifications. It resembled nothing so much as a long metal tube rotating slowly along its central axis. A space station? The spin would provide an artificial gravity, she thought.

"How big is it?" she asked.

"Fifteen-point-three-two kilometers in length," Tuvok said. "One-point-six-one kilometers in diameter."

The Sperians certainly believed in working on a grand scale, she thought. As the end came into view, she realized with a touch of disappointment that it hadn't been finished; the end nearest to the *Voyager* hadn't been sealed for an atmosphere. What looked like bright yellow and red working lights glowed from deep inside. Perhaps survivors from the attack on the space city were hiding safely in there, she thought.

"Look at the size of that thing," she heard Harry breathe softly to himself.

"There are no life signs," Marta said. "I'm picking up a large energy flux inside."

Janeway nodded slowly, trying to puzzle it through. What she'd taken to be work lights showing from the open end had taken on a faint pulsating flicker: a power source indeed.

"What's causing it?" she asked.

"There appears to be a massive power generator working at full capacity," Marta said.

"Bring us alongside the tube, Mr. Paris," Janeway said. "I want a closer look."

She leaned forward. As Tom brought them around in front of the tube, she gazed down its length at a maelstrom of light and energy pulsating deep within. It reminded her of something from the Academy long, long ago. She frowned, trying to bring back the memory. It was something about an ultimate weapon, she thought. What class had it been in? Exobiotics? Xenophilosophy?

Chakotay said, "It seems, somehow, familiar—"

"I feel the same way," Janeway said. "I think it's from one of my xeno classes at the Academy, but I can't quite remember which one."

"In the twenty-third century," Tuvok said, "the *Starship Enterprise* encountered a cone-shaped device of similar dimensions which carved up planets and consumed them as fuel."

"That's right," Janeway said. It all came flooding back. "I remember now. It was part of Dr. Englehardt's lecture series on extragalactic civilizations. She speculated that this 'doomsday machine' originated in another galaxy—but couldn't it have come from the far reaches of the Delta Quadrant instead?"

Tuvok said, "Doubtful. That so-called doomsday machine left a clear trail of devastation which led toward the outer rim of our galaxy—and, assumably, into intergalactic space beyond."

Chakotay said, "They believed it originated in the Andromeda galaxy, if I remember correctly."

"That is right," Tuvok said. "However, we also know that our galaxy has had extragalactic visitations at least three times, so there may have been contact—perhaps even a technology exchange—between the makers of that 'doomsday machine' and the Sperians or whoever made this particular device."

"Captain," said Harry Kim, interrupting. "The distress call has stopped, but I've pinpointed its source. It's coming from a small ship approximately thirty-five hundred kilometers beyond the tube."

Janeway started to order a scan of the ship for life signs, but before she could, a brilliant white light filled the bridge. She raised her hands to shield her eyes from the intensity.

"Shields up!" she cried. "Red alert! Ensign Dvorak, begin spectral analysis——"

A second later a violent shock wave jolted the bridge. The brightness seemed to pulsate around her. She felt *Voyager*'s deck rock beneath her and had to steady herself against the navigator's console.

"There's a high-energy beam coming from inside the tube!" Marta called. "I'm reading massive power levels and a subspace disturbance——"

The dazzling light abruptly cut to a more normal level as someone—Harry Kim, she thought—adjusted the image controls for maximum contrast. Spots swam before her eyes, but she blinked rapidly and they began to fade. Everyone around her seemed dazed, but uninjured. All systems seemed to be functioning. It seemed the energy beam hadn't been directed at them.

Turning, she looked at the viewscreen again. A pulsating stream of energy, easily a kilometer wide, shot from the open end of the tube . . . the end they'd just crossed. They'd missed being caught in the beam by mere seconds, she thought uneasily. Her sixth sense had been right.

"It's hitting the space city behind us," Tuvok said.

"On screen," Janeway ordered.

Harry punched it up. The space city was disintegrating like an ice cube in boiling water. As she watched, what remained of the city's elaborate durasteel framework crumpled, then vaporized. Hundreds of globe-shaped compartments simply vanished in the space of a few heartbeats; others melted or burst apart in devastating explosions. The beam was like all the energy of a supernova channeled into one stream, she thought with mingled horror and fascination. There wasn't a thing she could do to stop the destruction.

CHAPTER

4

Mentally shaking herself awake, Janeway snapped, "Analysis, Mr. Tuvok!"

Tuvok said, "The discharge does not appear to be aimed. Except for its rotation, the tube has not moved a centimeter since it began firing. The space city's position is at fault."

"You called it a discharge. Explain."

"More accurately," Tuvok said, "it resembles the spill-off of a large energy buildup that has no place to dissipate naturally."

"Are you saying it isn't a weapon?" she asked, feeling a little confused. If it wasn't a weapon, what could it be?

"Its destructive force is equal to that of a weapon," the Vulcan admitted. "However, further study is needed. The massive subspace disturbance that Ensign Dvorak noted suggests the device may have another as yet unknown function."

"What sort of maneuvering capabilities does it have?" she asked, returning to her seat. If it tried to turn and fire on them, she wanted to be prepared.

Marta said, "It has small maneuvering thrusters at either end, but nothing more. Considering its huge mass, we can run rings around it, Captain."

"Good to know. Keep an eye on it, Mr. Paris. If that thing begins to turn, I don't want *Voyager* caught in its beam."

"You can bet on it," he said.

"For now, move us back slowly, impulse power only," she said. "I want plenty of breathing room."

"Aye, Captain. No problem there." Tom made the necessary adjustments to the controls and *Voyager* began to back away. "Five thousand kilometers and holding."

The tube just kept firing and firing, seemingly without any rational purpose except to destroy. She glanced at a chronometer. Thirty-five seconds so far and still going strong. The energy being expended could have powered *Voyager* for months.

The device made no move to follow them; it continued to blast the space city, boiling away the metal and plastic, reducing it to a cloud of ionized gas. In a few more seconds, she thought, nothing would be left but useless debris.

She frowned, considering Tuvok's analysis. It begged the questions of why. Why would the Sperians build such a machine if it wasn't a weapon? If it was a weapon, why would they need to fight a war on such a scale? And why would they turn it on themselves?

Then she remembered the Borg and gave a small shudder. Perhaps there were times when civilized

42

people had need of such weapons. At the height of the conflict with the Borg, with half the fleet destroyed and morale at its lowest, Starfleet would have mortgaged its future for this machine.

She glanced at a chronometer. The tube had only been firing for a minute and a half, but it seemed a lot longer. *I would have estimated at least five minutes*, she thought. The amount of sheer sustained firepower was incredible, far greater than anything she'd ever seen before.

Then, just as quickly as it began, the blast ended. The lights inside the tube slowly dimmed to a dull flickering reddish orange. Silence stretched through the bridge, broken only by the alarm klaxon of the red alert.

"Shut that off," she said. "Resume yellow alert." They didn't seem to be in any immediate danger, she thought.

"Is that advisable, Captain?" Tuvok asked even as he complied.

"We've seen no sign of hostile ships," she said. "We can keep out of the tube's way if it fires again. I see no need to maintain battle readiness." She found she'd been clenching the arms of her chair and forced herself to let go. She hadn't realized how tense she'd been the whole time the tube had been firing. It left her completely drained. She touched her brow and found it damp with sweat.

"It appears," Tuvok said, "that the tube depleted all of its stored energy in that one burst."

"That wasn't a burst," Tom Paris said, "that was an out-and-out attack!"

"What happened to the space city?" Janeway went on. "Is anything left?"

"It is completely gone," Tuvok said, studying the sensors. "Only scattered small debris remains."

"Use tractor beams to bring some of it into docking bay two," Janeway said. "I want a full analysis—structural and stress. Mr. Kim, what happened to that ship you were monitoring?"

"Uh, yes, Captain," he said quickly, checking his instruments. "It's still drifting. It wasn't caught in the tube's blast, though the shock waves threw it farther away."

"I have sensors locked on to it, now, Captain," Marta said. "It appears to be a small spaceship. It's moving slowly away from us; from the trajectory, it appears to have originated from the space city. Its hull is intact, although I'm reading minor structural damage. I show one life-form aboard. It's barely registering, however." She looked up. "The ship's present course will take it into the white dwarf's gravitational influence within six hours."

"Are we in tractor-beam range?"

"Not at present."

"Ahead quarter impulse power, Mr. Paris. Stay clear of the tube's mouth. Lock on to the small ship with a tractor beam as soon as you're able and bring it aboard docking bay two."

"Aye, Captain." Tom Paris moved to comply.

Janeway touched her comm badge. "Captain to Torres. We are bringing a shuttlecraft and some debris from the space city aboard. Assemble a team and check it out. I want your analysis by nineteen hundred hours." If anyone could make sense out of the alien's equipment, B'Elanna could. And perhaps that would provide her with a few answers.

"I'm on it, Captain," B'Elanna said quickly.

"Shall I have the transporter room beam the alien directly to sickbay?" Harry Kim asked.

"Not until we know whether it can live in our atmosphere," Janeway said. "Ensign Dvorak, what is the composition of its atmosphere?"

"Oxygen-nitrogen, with a touch of helium and hydrogen. It should be able to survive in our air mix."

Janeway touched her badge. "Captain to sickbay. Activate the emergency medical program."

The ship's holographic doctor responded at once: "Sickbay. I'm already activated, Captain. Please state the nature of the emergency."

"Doctor," said Janeway, "we are picking up an injured alien. Neelix has identified it as a Sperian. I am having it beamed directly to sickbay."

"Understood. Out."

With all the knowledge and computer genius available in the twenty-fourth century, Janeway thought with a trace of wry amusement, they still couldn't design a computer program with a decent bedside manner. Even so, the hologram had begun to grow on her. He—if it was the right word—had a certain measure of spunk.

"Now, Mr. Kim," she said, "you can beam the Sperian to sickbay."

Kes held a medical tricorder ready as transporter lights shimmered and a familiar high-pitched whine filled the air. An alien—a Sperian, Captain Janeway had called him—began to materialize on the diagnostic table before her.

"Beginning decontamination procedure," the doctor told her.

"Will that hurt him?" she asked.

"It shouldn't. It only goes after microorganisms such as bacteria, viruses, and photomorphs. There is always a risk of eliminating a helpful or symbiotic organism, but the screening process attempts to account for that."

When the Sperian finished materializing, the decontamination field shimmered over his body for a second longer, then vanished, too.

"It's safe now," the doctor said. "You can begin your scan."

Kes activated the tricorder and began a bioanalysis. The Sperian looked like no alien she had never seen before. In her time on the *Voyager* she had seen more different types of people than she'd ever dreamed of meeting, from humans to Vulcans to Kazon to Bajorans to dozens of others, but all of those had maintained a familiar humanoid appearance.

The Sperian, though, was something else. He had no eyes, ears, or nose that she could see, and his mouth was little more than a round hole filled with rings of triangular black teeth. Limp gray tendrils as big around as her little finger covered the top third of his head. He had two arms and two legs, each with three joints, and three fingers tipped with triangular black claws. Faint gray blotches patterned his round and leathery torso. He wore no clothing or ornamentation of any kind, perhaps because he had no secondary—or primary—sexual characteristics that she could see.

"Should he look like this?" she asked. He didn't look at all well to her.

"His respiration is faint, but that could be normal," the doctor said, studying his medical tricorder. "His irregular skin coloration is the result of natural pigmentation, which is also probably normal. I'd say yes, he should look like this."

"Then he is a male?"

"I see no reproductive organs inside or out. Perhaps he is a worker-drone of some kind. On Earth, some insect colonies function like that, with sterile, almost asexual members to perform the menial tasks."

Kes leaned forward and placed her hand before the Sperian's open mouth. He was breathing slowly. So many teeth, she thought, counting three rows, each progressively smaller the farther in you went.

"Blood pressure," the doctor went on, still studying his tricorder, "is also low, but that may be normal. Brain activity minimal, but present; perhaps he is in a coma or the Sperian equivalent. No broken bones. All internal organs appear intact. No evidence of external abrasions or lacerations."

"In short," Kes said, "there's nothing wrong with him."

"Except for the minimal brain activity, yes."

"Any diagnosis?"

"Post-traumatic stress might be a good guess. If this species suffers from it."

She lowered her tricorder. "What can we do?" She'd seen plenty of wounds, but nothing like this before.

"Wait," the doctor said, "and see if he comes out of it on his own. Without a complete medical profile on his species, that's about all we can do at this time."

What a load of junk, B'Elanna Torres thought.

Debris littered the floor of the huge, misshapen docking bay two. As she picked her way among the slagged metal and plastic ship at the far end, she couldn't help but think what a waste of time all this poking about was. So much of the equipment was damaged beyond recognition, she'd never be able to figure out what it was used for, let alone how it had worked.

"Get stress fracture readings," she said to Peter Dawson, the tall blond ensign to her right. To Ensign Li Wong, the dark-haired woman on her left, she said, "Take metal samples for analysis."

"Yes, sir," both said, splitting off to examine different bits of shattered bulkhead.

B'Elanna continued to pick her way through the rubbish. Then, rounding a particularly large hunk of half-vaporized bulkhead, she came upon one of those quirky little oddities that she'd always found kept life from getting boring: a small, square instrument panel buried in a two-meter-tall chunk of gray durasteel bulkhead glowed with a steady yellow light. After all it had been through, she couldn't believe it was still functioning.

"Hello there," she whispered, studying the tricorder in her hand. Things had definitely taken an interesting turn, she thought. What was it a control *for?* She circled the bulkhead slowly, looking it over.

The edges were all melted. On the other side, on what had been the inner wall of one of the spherical compartments, another panel of lights glowed, this one a pale blue. Both seemed to be controls for something, she thought with growing excitement. Her tricorder revealed a schematic of the circuits and wires buried deep inside the wall . . . and they seemed to be complete.

If this circuit went here, and that one connected there, the controls would be operated by inserting her fingers into these three depressions and turning, she rapidly deduced. It seemed simple enough.

Taking a deep breath, she clipped the tricorder to her belt and stuck her fingers into the three holes. Here goes nothing, she thought, and she gave the panel a quick turn to the right.

She caught her breath and waited. Nothing happened. She counted to ten slowly, then exhaled. Nothing at all.

It's probably just the light that's still working, she thought with a measure of disappointment. After all this piece of bulkhead had been through, it was amazing that anything still functioned.

Then she tried twisting the panel to the left. Something clicked faintly into place, and she felt a momentary thrill as machinery whirred deep inside the bulkhead. Suddenly seams appeared as the metal began to split in two.

She stepped back, hand dropping to the phaser on her belt. What was that? What had she activated?

Suddenly a small round hatchway swung open with a squeal of protest. She allowed herself to relax with a quick bark of laughter. Just an airlock, she thought.

Bending, she peered through the hole at the far side of the docking bay. Li Wong had turned at the noise and was staring at her. B'Elanna gave a quick wave, then stood.

An access hatch to nowhere. It had probably connected one of the silver globes to one of the passageways. She gave a snort of amusement. Well, what else would you expect to find in a bulkhead? It was miracle enough that anything here still worked.

Raising her tricorder again, she continued toward the small spaceship. There seemed little of interest in any of the debris, she thought. She'd learned some of the basics of their engineering principles from how the hatch and its power supply were put together. The spaceship would tell her more.

She reached the spaceship and circled it once, studying the readouts on her tricorder. Roughly four meters in diameter, it was little more than a thin durasteel shell with rudimentary thrusters and a low-level life-support system. It wasn't so much a shuttle or an escape pod, she realized, as an engineer's vessel. It had two remote-controlled arms in front whose sole function had to be manipulating building materials in space. Its pilot must have been out working when the tube-weapon destroyed his home base.

It only took her a minute to find the hatch controls: three holes set close together in the hull, exactly like the airlock in the bulkhead. Sperians certainly didn't believe much in safety features, she thought. Such a design never would have been approved by Klingons or humans. Inserting her thumb and first two fingers into the holes, she twisted until she heard a low click.

A second later a round hatch on the underbelly of the ship popped open with a faint hiss of escaping air.

There weren't steps or rungs of any kind, so she levered herself up and in with a low grunt. Good thing she kept working out, she told herself.

The smell hit her first: a sour reek of alien sweat. She wrinkled her nose in disgust. A very primitive air-filtration system, she thought. She'd seen the Sperian's distress call, and suddenly she remembered he didn't have a nose . . . and with no sense of smell, he'd have no need to worry about offending odors.

Balancing on the balls of her feet, she used her tricorder to try to locate a light source. There wasn't one of those, either. No eyes, she reminded herself. But what about the amber light for the airlock? It probably came that way, she thought. They must have purchased the airlocks as whole units, then installed them . . . which explained why it still worked even after the blast.

She found the controls to open the viewport, and the docking bay's bright light flooded in. Slowly B'Elanna turned, looking around. Everything was gray and plain. She saw no decorations, no words, no pictures, and gave a little shudder. It was like a prison cell, she thought. She would have gone crazy if she had to work eight hours a day in a vessel like this one.

From a design standpoint, she thought, studying her tricorder again, it was a primitive craft: no artificial gravity, no food or sanitary facilities. A plastic harness dangled in the center of the cabin; the pilot must have hung inside it, suspended over the controls. From there he could also manipulate the ship's external arms through sophisticated waldoes.

The large viewport occupied one wall, and the thruster controls took up the wall to the right, and behind her sat a round viewscreen and communications console. Nothing here came close to matching Starfleet technology, though there were a number of similarities in basic design.

The smell was starting to make her faintly nauseated. She took a few more tricorder readings, but turned up nothing of interest. Since there didn't seem much more point in looking around further, she climbed back out, sealed the hatch, and called her team together.

"Anything interesting to report?" she asked.

"Material analysis shows nothing unusual," Dawson said. "It's durasteel, with just a trace more cadmium and rhodinium than Starfleet uses. Everything has a slightly higher than normal radiation level, but proximity to the white dwarf would account for that."

B'Elanna nodded. "True. Ensign Wong?"

"Everything has stress fractures," she said softly. "It's consistent with being blasted apart."

"Then everything checks out exactly as we expected," B'Elanna said. "All right, report back to Engineering. I'll let the captain know we can dump this junk." She couldn't even see much reason to keep the ship, unless the alien they'd taken aboard wanted it back for some reason.

There must be something I'm missing, Captain Janeway mused, staring at the tube. With no evidence of an outside invasion force, she could only assume the Sperians had built it here for their own reasons.

But how could they create such a machine, then allow it to destroy them? If they had simply pointed the tube a little bit away from their space city, its discharge would have passed harmlessly by. Either they were colossally stupid (not likely in a race advanced enough to build such a machine) or something else, something she had missed, was to blame for what had happened.

"Captain," said Marta Dvorak, "you wanted me to let you know of any changes in the tube's status."

"What have you got?" she asked. Perhaps the answer lay at hand.

"I'm reading another power buildup inside the tube."

"Confirmed," Tuvok said.

Janeway looked from one to the other. "How long has it been since the energy discharge?"

"One-point-two-five hours," Tuvok said.

"We must assume it's going to fire again," she said, thoughts racing ahead to the damage another such discharge might cause. "At the current rate of power regeneration, how long do we have?"

Marta Dvorak ran a few quick computations. "Best estimate . . . approximately five and a half hours, Captain."

Five and a half hours until that mammoth blast comes again, Janeway thought. That gave them some time to study and plan.

Next blast she'd be ready.

CHAPTER

5

"AHA!" SAID NEELIX, WAVING THE BUTCHER KNIFE HE'D been using to cut the *pagaloaf* at Paul Fairman. "Just the man I want to see!"

He had been half watching the doors to the galley ever since the disaster with the *paga* stew. The ventilators had long ago cleared out the smoke; now only a faint lingering odor remained. Fortunately few crewmen had noticed; those who had seemed to have chalked it up as just another bizarre side effect of real cooking.

Neelix had known Fairman would be back, however. For one thing, this was the only place to get lunch, and for another, Fairman still wanted that portable power supply.

"Your so-called lunch tried to kill me," Fairman said, picking up a tray. "You never warned me it could blow up!"

"I told you to stir it."

"Damm it, Neelix, I'm a mercenary, not a chef!"

Neelix snorted. "You can say that again."

"Now, about that portable power supply—"

"One moment, please," Neelix said, and humming softly, he hurried to the back of the kitchen and gave a couple of quick stirs to tonight's dinner: demi-smoked *phu* with *yerma* sauce. The bright yellow *phu*, which had been bubbling toward the top of its pot, settled down and once more began to let off its pale orange smoke.

When he returned to Fairman, the human had a more properly repentant look on his face. "I'm sorry if I screwed up lunch," he said. "I—I just panicked."

Neelix gestured grandly with the butcher knife. "Not at all," he said. That was all he really wanted to hear, he thought: you had to lead humans to everything, it seemed sometimes. "It could have happened to anyone. Cooking is a lot trickier than it looks."

"About the power supply—"

"Yes, yes," Neelix said. "About that power supply. What exactly do you want it for, anyway?"

"It's a surprise."

"A surprise?" That piqued his interest. He'd always been fond of surprises.

"All I can tell you," Fairman said with a wink, "is that it'll really raise morale."

"Just yours, or the whole crew's?"

Fairman looked hurt. "Everyone's," he said.

"Well," Neelix said, "I've always been a gambler at heart. If it's for the good of the crew, you know I'm all for of it. I'll do my best," he promised, "but I must warn you, it may end up being expensive."

"You're welcome to anything I have," Fairman promised.

Neelix put his butcher knife down and gave Fairman a quick hug. "It's nice to see someone being generous for a change," he said. "That was exactly the sort of spirit he liked to engender in the crew.

"I try," Fairman said.

Everything seemed to be under control, so Neelix picked up a plate and began spooning up Fairman's lunch. As a reward for such generosity, he gave Fairman an extra large slice of the *pagaloaf* smothered in a pungent Drayonian red sauce.

"Nothing to report, Captain," Chakotay said calmly. "Long-range scans aren't picking up anything yet."

Janeway nodded; she hadn't expected any news yet.

"Carry on, Commander," she said. "I'll be in sickbay checking up on our visitor if you need me."

"Yes, Captain," he said.

Janeway entered the turbolift and stated her destination. She couldn't get her thoughts off the destruction she'd just witnessed. As the turbolift whisked her toward the proper deck, she began to turn over the questions posed by the tube-cannon. Chief among them remained *why*. She was missing something, she felt. But what was it that bothered her?

She had a feeling it would come to her if she slept on it—but she wasn't sure she had that much time. Perhaps B'Elanna's evaluation of both the debris and the Sperian's spaceship would shed light on the situation.

And there still remained the tube itself to examine.

She'd left Tuvok and Ensign Dvorak analyzing it down to its smallest particle when she left the bridge. Perhaps they could shed some light on the whys of its existence.

When she walked into sickbay, she found Kes and the ship's holographic doctor standing beside one of the medical tables. The Sperian, looking gray and thin except for his bulb-shaped torso, lay still as death while Kes lowered a scanning bar over his chest. Glowing faintly, the bar glided up the alien's body, feeding reams of information to the tricorder in the doctor's hands. Even the tendrils on the Sperian's head hung limp and unmoving, Janeway noticed. Then she saw him take a slow breath through the mouth in the middle of his head.

"How is he?" she asked with some concern.

"His condition appears stable," said the doctor.

"What's wrong with him?"

"I'm not sure," he said.

"Our best guess," Kes broke in, "is some form of severe stress-induced shock."

"At least, that's what I'd say if he were human," the doctor said. "With his alien physiology, I can't tell for certain. It could be something entirely different."

"Has he regained consciousness at all?" Janeway leaned forward, studying his face. She hated to be provincial, but she wished he had eyes—she'd always managed to find a commonality with species who shared the sense of sight.

"No," the doctor said. "It's as though he willfully shut down his brain. If there were a head trauma of any kind, I'd say he was in a coma. What happened to him? Did he suffer anything unusual?"

"He watched thousands of his race die."

The doctor paused, but didn't look surprised.

"That might well account for it," he said.

"Is there anything you can do to bring him around?" Janeway said. If she could only question him, she might begin to find some of the answers, she thought. "Aren't there any stimulants you can try?"

"I'm not going to risk murdering a patient by trying a random assortment of stimulants," the doctor said. "This isn't the twenty-first century, Captain."

"We've been trying to figure out how his body works," Kes said quickly. "The doctor has pretty much mapped out his circulatory system. We were about to start on his central nervous system."

"But isn't there something you can do now?" she pressed. "It's important, Doctor."

"My best advice, based on the experiences of more than forty top physicians and the cumulative medical data collected by the Federation over the last hundred years, is to do nothing for the moment because nothing is noticeably physically wrong."

"But he may be dying!"

"True," the doctor said, "but he may also be entering a period of extended hibernation wherein his body will repair whatever physical or psychological damage it has received. Or this may be the normal sleep-state for his kind. Or there may be still other possibilities. We simply don't know. Without extensive research I cannot offer anything beyond a tentative hypothesis at this point, and that is stress-induced shock. The Sperian's physical makeup and internal organs are like nothing I have ever seen before."

Reluctantly, Janeway nodded. If he couldn't do anything, he couldn't do anything; she'd just have to wait. "Very well," she said, "but I want to be kept informed of any changes in his status."

"Your instructions are noted," the hologram said. He looked down at his patient. "Since I don't require sleep, I was planning to monitor him around the clock anyway."

"Carry on," Janeway said. She stared down at the Sperian's gray, eyeless face and felt a twinge of sorrow for all he'd suffered. Shock-induced trauma, it had to be that. He'd watched thousands of his kind die . . . friends, coworkers, perhaps even his family. A human would have felt the same thing—shock, horror, loss, and guilt. Guilt for surviving where so many others had died.

She turned and started for the door. It was going to be a long day, she thought.

CHAPTER

6

AT SEVENTEEN HUNDRED HOURS, CAPTAIN JANEWAY CONvened the senior officers for a meeting. No more ships had appeared; the tube continued its power buildup on schedule. If Tuvok's and Ensign Dvorak's estimates proved accurate—and she had every reason to believe they would—the tube would fire again in another hour and ten minutes.

She scanned the grave faces around the table. B'Elanna and Chakotay sat to her left; Harry Kim, Tom Paris, and Tuvok sat to her right. Only Kes and Neelix were missing, and she expected them any moment.

The doors suddenly whisked opened and Neelix appeared, wheeling a small metal cart with a covered lid. He wore a neon green chef's hat and an orange-and-blue striped apron over an equally loud orange one-piece suit. Kes, in a blue and black jumpsuit, brought up the rear, carrying plates and silverware.

"What is the meaning of this, Mr. Neelix?" Janeway asked, letting a faint note of surprise and annoyance creep into her voice. She didn't like the little surprises that he constantly seemed to be springing on her at meetings.

"I'm sorry we're a little late, Captain," he said, "but I'm afraid it's my own fault: the *yerma* sauce came out a little too watery and I had to prepare another batch."

"I meant—this!" she gestured at the cart and his hat and apron.

"Dinner, of course, Captain." He whisked the lid from the cart, revealing a deep metal basin filled with brightly colored vegetables in a creamy green sauce. "The Verosan goulash I've been promising for so long." He gave her a wink. "It's one of my specialties, you know."

"Mr. Neelix," she began with a sign, "this is supposed to be an officer's meeting, not a banquet—"

"Believe me, I know what you mean," he said. Kes began setting plates, forks, and spoons out in front of everybody. "But I don't consider it an imposition," Neelix went on. "It's more important that you eat. Don't worry, I'll clean everything up afterward."

"Who is watching the galley?" Chakotay asked.

"Paul Fairman volunteered," Neelix said.

"Fairman *volunteered?*" Chakotay asked. Janeway heard the surprise in his voice and concurred: when they'd gone over the Maquis roster, Fairman had been one of the few they'd had little hope for. He'd been a mercenary, fighting with the Maquis for money rather than politics, and Chakotay had him pegged as a potential subversive and troublemaker. Fortunately

61

he'd kept a low profile so far, doing his assigned work but not one bit more than the bare minimum expected of him.

"That's right," Neelix said. "A delightful fellow, really. Such potential. I've been thinking of training him as a backup chef."

Chakotay laughed and shook his head. "Glad to hear it," he said. "If you can make an honest man of him, I'm all in favor of it."

"About this food—" Janeway began. Then she sniffed.

Now that the spicy odor of the goulash had begun to pervade the room, she had to admit it did smell appetizing—and much more so than most of Neelix's recent concoctions. She glanced around the table. Everyone had begun to stare at the food with more than a measure of interest, even Tuvok, though it was hard to tell with a Vulcan. Then she felt her own stomach give a faint hungry rumble. Perhaps, she thought, she could make an exception and have a dinner meeting—just this once.

"Very well," she said, "since you've gone to so much trouble, you may proceed. But I don't want to make a habit of dinner meetings."

"Of course not, Captain," Neelix said soothingly. "It's just that in times of crisis everyone needs to keep their strength up, I always say." He wheeled his cart over to her, ladled out a large portion of stew, and stepped back appreciatively. "Give it a try," he said.

She picked up her fork, speared a small, round, bright yellow globule, and held it up, turning it this way and that. It reminded her of a yellow onion, she thought. After a moment's hesitation, she popped it into her mouth and chewed.

It burst like a balloon, flooding her mouth with a warm flavorful juice. The taste reminded her of cinnamon at first, but then as she chewed, a hint of almonds and honey appeared. She closed her eyes for a second, savoring it. When she opened them again, everyone was looking at her. She felt a moment's embarrassment; she wasn't one to gush over food, after all. But she'd never had anything quite like this before.

Neelix had a puppy-dog expression of eager antici- pation on his face.

"Delicious," she said after she swallowed. This was one of the few Neelix-prepared meals she actually thought she'd enjoy to the fullest. It had to happen eventually, she thought: he'd found a food that was appealing to humans. "What did you say these yellow things are?"

He beamed. "Maga-berries, of course." Turning, he ladled a portion out onto Chakotay's plate, then proceeded around the table, lastly serving Kes and then himself. Finally he wheeled the cart out of the way, sat, and looked around the table expectantly. "Well—enjoy!"

One by one everyone tried the food. Janeway watched as face after face broke out in a smile: the maga-berries in particular seemed quite a hit.

Even Tuvok nodded. "Quite palatable," he said.

That, Janeway thought, had to be one of the highest compliments she'd ever heard a Vulcan pay to a meal. She'd once heard Tuvok refer to a four-nova restau- rant on Betazed as "sufficiently nutritious."

Finally, after everyone had finished, Janeway pushed aside her plate. "It's time to get down to business," she said, wiping the corners of her mouth. "We all saw that tube and what it can do. Current opinions? Chakotay."

"It *is* an amazing weapon," he said slowly, "built on a scale to pulverize planets. It is a testament to the space station's construction that it wasn't destroyed in the first blast."

"I agree," B'Elanna said. "Anything that destructive must be a prototype for an ultimate weapon of some kind."

"No, no, no," Neelix said. "That's simply not possible. I know the Sperians. They are so wrapped up in petty internal squabbles that they have no need for a weapon, ultimate or otherwise. Nobody bothers them—they are their own worst enemies."

"I must concur with Mr. Neelix," said Tuvok. "Logically, it's too big and ungainly to used in any sort of war; it would be destroyed before it could fire a single shot. *Voyager* would have no trouble keeping out of its way on maneuvering thrusters alone. And it doesn't seem to have been built to move outside of the Arbuk system—a strategically useless place to position it."

"Perhaps it's a prototype," Harry Kim suggested. Janeway nodded; she'd wondered about that herself.

"That theory does not stand logical scrutiny," Tuvok said. "An early prototype would be built to a much smaller scale. This device is the product of many years of work. It is clearly a final model. However, something has gone wrong either in the design or in its use: it is not functioning as intended or that space city would not have been destroyed. Thirteen thousand casualties is not acceptable in a test of a prototype weapon."

"That's assuming the Sperians built the tube," Chakotay said. "What if they didn't?"

Janeway glanced at him in surprise. That possibility hadn't even occurred to her.

Tuvok, though, had an answer ready: "Illogical. The tube must have been constructed in its current position. It has no warp capacity. It could not have originated outside of this system."

Chakotay turned to B'Elanna. "Our scans revealed small thrusters which can turn it slowly, but nothing else. Can you think of another way to move it?"

"Short of a tractor beam? No. Not unless you attached engines to it later—but I'd like to see warp engines built to move something of that mass and size!"

"Warp engines . . ." Janeway said. "Wasn't there a subspace distortion when it first began to fire?"

"Sure," Tom said. "It jolted the whole ship."

"What caused it?" she asked. She looked from face to face, but as she half expected, nobody had an answer, not even Tuvok. "We'll come back to that," she said. "Now, if we assume the tube has malfunctioned, what other use could it possibly have? What could it have been designed for?"

"Perhaps the answer to your second question will shed light on the first," Tuvok said.

"We'll learn more when the Sperian recovers," Janeway said. She didn't voice her thought, *If the Sperian recovers.* "Is it showing any signs of waking up, Kes?"

"Not yet," she said. "And the doctor feels he could be a worker-drone, like among Earth's bees."

"Interesting," Janeway said. "Meantime, what else have we learned? B'Elanna."

B'Elanna said, "I looked over the Sperian's ship as well as the debris in docking bay two. The ship was built for space construction. Its pilot was an engineer; the ship was equipped with waldoes. Our analysis of the debris showed nothing usual: just durasteel with a high cadmium content and a lot of melted plastic and wiring. About what you'd expect, considering what it went through."

"Any recommendations?"

"Jettison everything. It's not worth the space."

"Very well, see to it. But keep the Sperian's ship on board. He might want it back." When *he wakes up,* she silently added.

Neelix spoke up: "If you don't mind, Captain," he said, "I have a little free time after dinner. With your permission, I'd like to look through the debris before it's jettisoned. There might be something I can use."

"I doubt it," B'Elanna said. "It's half-melted rubble."

"One species' rubble is another species' treasure," he said.

"I see no harm in it," Janeway said. Neelix worked miracles with the materials he scavenged, she knew from experience; there was no telling what he might find useful. "Very well, Mr. Neelix, but have it done by twenty hundred hours."

"Thank you, Captain!" he said, beaming.

"Our priority must be finding out more about that tube before deciding what to do with it," Janeway said. "If there's a way to shut it off, I want to know about it. Recommendations?"

"Let me take a work party over to examine it more closely," B'Elanna said. "There are bound to be controls of some sort. I haven't seen anything here that surpasses Starfleet's current level of technology, so we should be able to figure everything out, given time."

Janeway nodded. That was good news, at least. "Do so. Take as many people as you need."

B'Elanna pushed back her chair. "I'll get right on it," she said.

"Dismissed," Janeway said, also rising. "Mr. Tuvok, if you would remain?"

"Of course, Captain," he said.

When the others had filed out and the doors closed, Janeway went around to where Tuvok sat. He watched her with no trace of emotion, yet she knew he must be curious. In his position, she would have been.

She sat on the edge of the table next to him and took a deep breath, trying to gather her thoughts. *I'm only putting it off,* she thought suddenly. *Tuvok deserves better than that.* This was a difficult thing to ask of any Vulcan, she knew, but she couldn't see any other way to reach the alien.

"Tuvok, we've known each other a long time," she began, "and we've been through a lot—"

"I believe I can anticipate what you are going to say, Captain," he said, looking her in the eyes. "We need to know more about the tube, and we need to know more about the Sperians and what caused the damage in their space city. Indeed, considering what happened here, establishing communications with the Sperian must logically become a priority."

"Quite right," she said. "Then you know what I am proposing."

He inclined his head. "You want me to initiate a mind-meld with the Sperian."

"Exactly." She wished she could have thought of a better way to reach the Sperian, but there didn't seem to be any at hand.

"It is a deeply personal sharing of one's self, Captain," he said slowly. "Not only will I gain access to the Sperian's mind, but he will gain a measure of access to mine. What he feels, I will feel. If his mind has been damaged, that damage may well affect me. And, of course, there is always a risk to both of us when we attempt to communicate in such a direct manner: we do not know the mental capabilities of his race."

"I know how risky and how personal a thing this is," she said, meeting his gaze. "That is why it must be your decision and yours alone."

He stood and folded his arms behind his back. "I believe only one decision is possible. Logically, my own survival as well as the survival of this ship and crew may depend on achieving communication with the Sperian. Therefore I will attempt it."

"When?"

"In one hour. I need time to ready myself mentally, since I have no idea how the Sperian's mind works. Should anything go wrong, I must be prepared. The ship appears to be in no danger at present. With your permission . . . ?"

"Granted," she said.

She watched as he turned smartly and strode from the room. Janeway sighed. She'd known he would agree. Not for the first time, she wished she had a hundred more like Tuvok among her crew.

CHAPTER

7

NEELIX TOOK A DEEP BREATH, OFFERED KES HIS HAND, and together they strolled into docking bay two. "It looks a little like one of the rock gardens on Feldersk Four," he said idly. All the towering, half-melted pieces of bulkhead had a weathered look if you squinted. "All it needs is a pink sky, a warm summer breeze, and half a dozen moons."

"It sounds beautiful," Kes said softly.

"I'll take you there sometime," he promised, stroking her arm. She would look so beautiful against a pink sky, he thought. He had to be the most fortunate person in the galaxy to have found her.

"What exactly are we looking for?" she asked.

"Anything and everything!" He forced his gaze from her wide eyes and scanned the docking bay for any interesting or unusual bits of salvage. "There's no telling where something useful will be hidden, I always say."

70

"Is there anything in particular we need?"

"Not really." He traced the line of her chin with one finger. He had never known anyone so beautiful before. Her hair, her skin, her smile—sheer perfection. "I only have eyes for you, you know."

"Oh, Neelix!" she laughed happily. "You're wonderful. But really, what do you want to find? How can I help?"

"Well . . ." He stopped and surveyed the ruined pieces of the space city a bit more critically. "Food is always the highest priority, but I don't think there's much chance of that here. Look for anything that can be used or recycled in some way. Sheet metal, self-contained storage vessels, that sort of stuff."

"How about that?" She pointed.

He followed her finger toward a glowing instrument panel set in one of the pieces of bulkhead twenty meters ahead.

"Very interesting," he said, squinting at it. "Let's take a look!"

Still holding hands, they headed over. Up close, it looked less impressive, Neelix thought. It was little more than a twisted section of bulkhead with a round hatch that had somehow popped open.

"It's just a Sperian airlock," he said with a trace of disappointment. Then he brightened. "The instrument panel is still functioning, though, which means it must have its own power source . . . and I can always use one of those!"

"What for?" Kes asked.

He gave her a wink. "It's going to be a surprise. But I hear it will definitely boost the whole crew's morale!" Craning his head this way and that, he examined both sides of the airlock, then the control panel's casing. "It's going to take me an hour to get this thing out," he said. "You know what that means, don't you?"

Kes giggled. "Just enough time for—"

"The entire Pegrina Mating Chant!" he finished. He pulled a small tool kit from one pocket, unfolded it, and removed an magnetic spanner. He used the sharp end to pry the instrument panel out of the bulkhead, exposing half a dozen variously colored wires, several relay couplings, and a handful of Sperian double-jointed lug nuts.

Kes, he saw, had seated herself cross-legged before him when his back was turned. "Ready," she said with a grin.

"The whole thing?" he asked.

"From start to finish!"

"Very well." Neelix cleared his throat. Then, as he unfixed the lugs and began to strip the wires away from the power couplings, he began to sing the first of the two thousand, two hundred and twenty-two stanzas:

The thousand days of love are shining through
     your eyes—
The thousand nights of love are beating in my
     heart—
The first day comes on feet of clay—
     Ai! Newly chosen are we!
The first night comes on wings of air—
     Ai! So light of heart are we!
The thousand days of love—

* * *

"Any progress, Doctor?" Captain Janeway asked. She'd stopped by the sickbay immediately after her talk with Tuvok to get an update. If only the Sperian would regain consciousness, she thought, she could spare her first officer the possible trauma of a bad mind-meld. For him to take an hour to ready himself mentally, she knew he expected the worst from the experience.

The doctor harrumphed a bit disapprovingly. "I'm afraid not, Captain," he said. "It's barely been two hours since your last visit. There haven't been any changes in the Sperian's condition, nor do any seem likely in the immediate future. As I told you, I will update you the moment there's the slightest change."

"How are you doing on mapping his central nervous system?"

"I've finished. I was just about to start on the digestive system in case he needs nutrients of some kind."

Janeway nodded; things were proceeding about as she had expected. If nothing else, a holographic doctor followed medical procedures by the book.

She took his arm. "Doctor, may I talk with you in your office?" she asked. She thought it best to talk to him alone, out of the earshot of any crewman who might walk in. Perhaps, if he knew the seriousness of the situation, he might find a way to speed up the alien's recovery.

"Certainly." The doctor turned and led the way to the small cubicle in the center of sickbay. Inside, instrument panels glowed and monitors gave soft bleeps as they watched over the Sperian.

Janeway closed the door after them. "I'm afraid I don't like the situation we're in," she said softly. "We're in a system with a devastated space city, a machine gone amok and throwing off huge blasts of energy at regular intervals, and no witnesses to say what really happened except an unconscious alien. If more Sperians show up, they're going to take one look at us and reach the rather obvious conclusion that we are responsible for the damage."

"I understand your point," the doctor said, "but I fail to see—"

"I *need* that Sperian awake. I *need* him able to communicate. Not only for the safety of this ship, but to let others of his kind know what's going on with their device so they can stop it if we're unable to do so. Do you understand the severity of this situation?"

She looked into his eyes and saw a softening of his features. He might only be a computer program, she thought, but he was more than the sum of his parts. He certainly reacted more like a man than some of the humans she'd known. And she'd noticed that the longer he ran, the more human his responses became . . . almost as if he were learning to be alive from watching everyone around him.

"There is one thing I haven't tried," he admitted.

"What?"

"His blood is copper-based, like a Vulcan's. We have several Vulcan psychotropic drugs aboard because of Lieutenant Tuvok's presence on the ship. They stimulate mental activity. I could try one of them."

"Do so!" she said.

"But," he went on, "he may have a bad reaction . . . or no reaction at all."

"The longer we're here," she said softly, "the greater the chance for an incident with the Sperians. Do you think the drug will kill him?"

"No," he said. "I don't think it will do anything at all in his bloodstream."

"Then try it."

"Very well." Leaving his office, the doctor retrieved a hypospray, crossed to a small cabinet, and removed a vial containing a pale green fluid. "Tetsorum D," he said. Carefully he measured out a dose, then turned to the bed where the Sperian lay.

Janeway followed. If there were any justice in the universe, she thought, this would work—no matter how long the odds.

The Sperian lay quietly, the tendrils on his head limp and unmoving, his mouth open. His breath sounded like a fluted whistle, low but regular. Lights on the monitoring device over his chest glowed in greens and ambers.

The doctor hesitated. "I'm still not convinced this is in the best interests of the patient," he said.

"You said it wouldn't kill him."

"I said I didn't *think* it would kill him."

"Doctor," she said, "if there's any real chance of doing him harm, do not use the drug. I'm not here to pressure you into committing murder. I'm not here to urge you to use all of the resources at your disposal to find an answer as rapidly as possible. Our situation here is serious, but not yet grave. If we have to, we *will* try something else." Like a mind-meld with Tuvok, she mentally added.

The doctor nodded. "I estimate the chances of the drug killing him at approximately nine hundred and sixty thousand to one against. I believe that falls within the parameters of an acceptable risk." He leaned forward and injected the Sperian in the side with the hypospray. "However," he said, "the chances of the drug helping him remain at a little over a hundred thousand to one against."

Janeway leaned forward, her breath catching in her throat. The medical readings changed slightly as she watched—a tiny flutter, then nothing. One of the tendrils on his head stirred faintly. Was it the start of something more? The tension started to rise inside her. *Come on,* she thought. *You can do it.*

But nothing more happened. The readouts remained low but stable. The tendrils on his head hung limp and unmoving. His breath continued its faint whistle. *No change.*

She couldn't help but feel a twinge of disappointment. Was that all? The doctor had worked miracles so many times in the past, she'd half expected one now.

But perhaps the drug took a while. "How long until we know if it worked?" she asked softly.

"We already do," the doctor said gently. He touched her arm. "I'm sorry, Captain. We had a few seconds of elevated brain activity, but then it fell back to normal. We can't expect anything more than that."

"Is an increased dose potentially helpful?"

"No," he said bluntly, "and I'm not even going to try. I stretched to the limits of my programming to give him that much. In time he may recover on his own—and I'm afraid that's his best hope, unless my study of his anatomy turns up something grotesquely wrong that I missed in my preliminary examinations."

"And what are the odds of that," she whispered, already knowing the answer.

"Almost none."

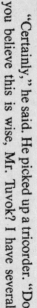

CHAPTER 8

TUVOK TOOK QUICK STOCK OF HIMSELF BEFORE STEPPING into the sickbay. He had prepared himself as best he could to mind-meld with the Sperian, going through a series of age-old Vulcan mental exercises. All children on Vulcan learned to martial their mental energies and focus their concentrations in such a manner. It was essential when dealing with illogical and completely alien species.

The ship's holographic doctor approached when he walked in. "Can I help you, Mr. Tuvok?" he asked.

"The captain has asked me to initiate a mind-meld with the Sperian," he said, "and I have agreed. Please monitor my condition throughout the joining, Doctor."

"Certainly," he said. He picked up a tricorder. "Do you believe this is wise, Mr. Tuvok? I have several

78

databases on Vulcan physiology to draw upon, and they stress the hazards of mind-melding with unconscious, unwilling, completely unfamiliar, and possibly brain-damaged subjects."

"I am well aware of the dangers involved, Doctor," Tuvok said. "I have taken all due precautions."

"Very well, then. I wish you success."

"Thank you." Tuvok approached the unconscious Sperian and cleared his thoughts. Vulcan mental disciplines, second nature to him, automatically cleansed his mind of emotions such as fear, apprehension, and nervousness. Logic and order held sway. Emotions, he knew, were the enemy of logic, the little deaths that chipped away at the inner tranquillity that all Vulcans strived to attain.

He looked into the alien's strangely featureless face and wondered how different his perceptions would be without senses like sight. The tendrils had to supply something akin to it, he thought.

He allowed his cool analytical gaze to chart the topography of the Sperian's head, and he began to plan how he would touch it, right hand *here*, left hand *there*, and how they would join.

Slowly he extended his right hand and felt the alien's cool gray skin. His fingertips tingled faintly as he sought the consciousness trapped within. Yes, he could sense it now, the turbulent, jumbled thoughts of an active subconscious mind, the chaotic disorder of undisciplined thought processes. He extended his left hand, probing, feeling, learning.

"Our minds are one," he whispered, pushing deeper into the consciousness. "Our thoughts are one." He sought mutual ground, experiences they had both

79

shared, any commonality that could help bridge the transition from two separate minds to one consciousness. "Our senses are joining. We are one."

Numbers. He found a shared appreciation of mathematics, an aesthetic sense that included the precise sweep of lines and curves and mathematical formulas of geometry, the purity of numbers, the soothing simplicity of analytical algorithms.

His name is Sozoas. He is an engineer for the Tech Faction. He has the answers we seek.

Tuvok felt his heart beginning to slow, matching the Sperian's beat for beat. They were becoming attuned to one another, he felt. In Sozoas he had found a like intellect, a being who appreciated logic and order, though he had never had formal training in either.

He pressed deeper. He felt the surge of blood in both their veins now, heard the whisper of air in both their lungs, felt the cool unyielding surface of the medical table beneath the Sperian's back.

We are one, he thought.

My thoughts are your thoughts—

Our bodies are one—

Our minds are joined—

Our thoughts—

The transition was subtle, like a slide down a greased chute, faster and faster, an unstoppable journey through images and emotions that were not his, but somehow belonged to him.

The hatching creche—

Bonding into the Tech Faction—

Training at Starfleet Academy—

Standing beneath the pale sun of Vulcan—

The union was unlike anything he had ever felt before, neither birth-sharing nor mind-meld, but a little bit of each. One second he was an outsider looking in, the next he was a larger whole, no longer Tuvok or Sozoas, but something new, something greater than either had been.

It was as though he had lived two completely different lives in completely different worlds and only just awakened to the fact. Symbiosis, he thought suddenly. It was a word and a concept at once alien and familiar. He explored his new body, four hands, four legs, two heads, two torsos. His tendrils imaged the textures of the room around him, the vibrations of sound, the weave of fabric, the smooth perfection of polished steel and glass and plastic.

Where am I?

His two eyes opened. His head turned as he studied the curtained-off section of the room Kes had prepared for him.

Voyager.

Safe.

He swung two of his legs around to the floor. The Tuvok extension moved with him, helping him up, a precisely balanced part of his body, at once wholly new and wholly familiar.

A strange place.

Duty.

His mission.

Logically, he must find a Faction leader and explain the situation.

Captain Janeway?

Leader Janeway.

His Sozoas extension sat up, swept aside the curtain, and with the Tuvok extension's help, strode toward the door. Colors now filled the world, part of him mused. He didn't understand the logic of it, but they intrigued him. Part of him had never suspected their existence, but now they seemed natural as he regarded them through his Vulcan eyes, just as the contour-shapes with which his stems mapped the room seemed at once strange yet reassuringly familiar.

A creature appeared before him, blocking his way. One of his senses registered it as a smooth object, with no more texture than polished durasteel plating. Another of his senses registered, brown eyes, pale skin, pink lips, and a strange unround body that looked somehow proper on those long, straight legs. The ship's doctor.

A fellow crewman.

A Faction-Friend.

"Friend Doctor," he said, the two tongues in his maw making the words half a twitter. He switched to his other mouth, the one in his Vulcan part. "I must find Leader Janeway and make my report to the Faction."

"You are not going anywhere yet, Tuvok," he said. "Listen to me. Something is wrong. You are still in the mind-meld. You need to release the Sperian."

Wrong?

An alien.

Tuvok.
An extension of me.

Mind-meld?

The Sperian.

Sozoas. Another extension of me.

He felt a growing impatience: when he tried to step around Friend Doctor, he blocked his way.

"Mr. Tuvok," Friend Doctor said again, touching one of his four arms, the one with five fingers, "I cannot allow you to leave sickbay. You're locked in a mind-meld with the Sperian. Let him go, Tuvok."

Mind-meld.

Separateness.

It cannot be allowed.

Slowly, silently, he reached out his foremost arm and squeezed the doctor's shoulder with his three-fingered hand. That was the place, he knew, where nerves clustered in humans, making them vulnerable.

Nothing happened. The doctor should have slumped to the floor unconscious, he thought, and then he could have stepped over him and continued on to see the captain and make his report to the Faction. But nothing happened. Why didn't Friend Doctor fall?

"Tuvok?" the doctor said. "Can you hear me?"

"Let me pass," he said. "I must report to Leader Janeway."

Instead, the doctor took his three-fingered hand and gently tried to turn him back toward the medical table. He found the sensation odd. Was this a bonding moment? He hesitated, confused.

"Mr. Tuvok," the doctor said, looking into the Tuvok-self's eyes, "can you hear me? Say something to me, Mr. Tuvok. I want to talk to *Tuvok*."

"Why are you still standing?" he asked. It seemed a

logical enough question, he thought. Friend Doctor should have been lying on the floor unconscious, after all.

"Easy," Friend Doctor said. He had been fumbling with a device with his free hand. Now he touched that device to the Tuvok-self's neck.

Dizziness swept through the composite.

Fragmenting—

Sliding back—

"N-no—" he gasped through both mouths with all three tongues. Darkness rushed upon him like a living creature. "It—cannot—be—allowed—"

CHAPTER 9

B'ELANNA FINISHED CLAMPING DOWN THE SPACESUIT'S helmet and nudged the comm unit with her chin. A faint hiss of background static sounded in her ears, letting her know it was operational. Strange how comforting that sound could be in the emptiness of space, she thought. The diagnostic display showed all green: the suit was fully powered up and operational. She had twelve hours of air left. As she watched, the digital readout clicked off a minute: 11:59:00.

"Wong, Dawson, check in," she said.

"Ensign Wong, all systems green," Li Wong said.

"Ensign Dawson, all systems green," Peter Dawson said.

B'Elanna turned to look at them. In their white spacesuits with light thruster packs hooked to their backs, they looked nearly identical, she thought. The light had to hit the helmets just right or you couldn't see their faces through the tinted faceplates. She looked the same, she knew.

"Lieutenant, is this going to be an all-nighter?" Dawson asked.

"Could well be," B'Elanna said. "Do you have a problem with that?"

"No," Dawson said quickly. "Just asking, sir."

"Good." B'Elanna turned, her motions exaggerated in the spacesuit as she fought normal gravity in the airlock. "I'll cycle us through."

She pulled the switch that pumped out the air in the airlock. A slight hiss reached her even through the insulation of her spacesuit. When the amber light turned green, she activated the second switch and a door to the outside of the *Voyager* slid silently open.

She pulled herself out, then activated the thrusters on her back. Tiny jets ignited, pushing her silently away from the airlock. *Voyager* fell away behind her, to her left loomed the brilliant white sphere of the white dwarf star, filling a quarter of the sky. To the left, about the size of the moon as seen from Earth, hung a bright ruby-colored disk, the red giant. Halfway between them, rolling end over end, bathed in their white and red glows, lay the Sperian's ultimate weapon.

A little less than an hour until it fired again, she thought. Well, she'd see about that. When she found the controls, she'd shut it down fast enough.

She glanced back. Dawson and Wong had followed her, also using the tiny thrusters on their backs to fly.

She gave hers another two-second burst, accelerating slightly toward the tube.

"We'll start at the near end," she said, "and fly down its length. I'll take the top, Dawson can take my left, and Wong, you can have the right. We'll form a triangle so we can see the whole of the tube as well as each other."

"What exactly do you want us to look for?" Li asked.

"A control room or anything else out of the ordinary," she said. "There must be an operations center for this thing."

"I just hope it's on the outside," B'Elanna heard Dawson mutter under his breath. She grinned a bit. "Don't forget we have an open mike, Mr. Dawson," she told him.

"Sorry, sir," he said.

"But your point is valid. If we don't find the control room outside, we'll have to look inside after the next blast."

It took five minutes to get to the tube and maneuver into position. B'Elanna kept glancing down at the flickering lights inside, which seemed to be growing more and more intense.

As if he'd read her thoughts, Ensign Harry Kim suddenly broke in on the radio channel they'd been using: "Lieutenant Torres," he said, "I thought you might like to know that we're still monitoring the energy buildup. You have forty-two minutes before the next discharge."

"Thanks," she said. "Keep an eye on it for me, Harry."

"No problem. Want us to transport you out before the blast?"

"If it gets to that, yes. It might be a good idea."

"Will do. Kim out."

She gave a low chuckle. Good kid, that one.

"All right," she barked, "assume your positions." She maneuvered to the top of the tube. Her ensigns flew to their places. When she could look down at the tube and see both of them from her peripheral vision, she gave a quick wave: "Let's go!"

She activated her thrusters and began to fly up the length of the tube. Below, the device's outer wall seemed to run forever, meter after meter of identical durasteel plate rotating slowly counterclockwise. It had been assembled from large rectangular panels, each welded seamlessly to the next with what looked like the finest job of duridium soldering she'd ever seen. Curiously, she saw no markings, no serial or parts numbers. It was as though the entire thing had been assembled by the robot workers they'd spotted earlier. Robots needed no such instructions; they kept all that information stored in the memory banks.

"Increase speed on my mark," she said. "Thirty klicks per hour."

"Roger," both Dawson and Wong said together.

"Mark," she said, firing her maneuvering thrusters in a pair of short bursts. She checked on the others. Wong had fallen a little behind, but caught up quickly.

More featureless kilometers of hull passed below. The durasteel plating started to blur. B'Elanna took a sip of water from the tube to the left of her mouth and refocused her attention. There had to be a control room, she thought. It was inconceivable that such a huge construction wouldn't have one.

Fifteen minutes later, when the end of the tube came up fast below, she used her thrusters to brake. No control room. It infuriated her. The Sperians had to be complete idiots. First no backup systems in the space city's bulkheads to prevent explosive decompression, and now no way to shut down this damn spinning war machine. Who had ever heard of such slipshod engineering? What had possessed the Sperians, anyway?

Perhaps Dawson was right and the control room was inside. She checked her chronometer. Sixteen minutes till the blast.

"Lieutenant," Dawson said suddenly, "I've found something." She heard more than a note of excitement in his voice.

Glancing over to where he had been, she found he'd vanished. She blinked. Where had he gone? Over the back end of the tube and out of her direct line of sight? But that would be crazy—the back end of the tube was open, and the blast was coming up fast.

"Where are you?" she asked.

"Just over the edge. There's a small access corridor built into the hull here. I've walked about two meters into it. I believe it's an airlock."

"Wait for me," B'Elanna said.

Turning, she fired her thrusters and zipped around the end of the tube. It looked exactly like the front end, completely open, and she could see a pulsating red-yellow glow of pent-up energy. Here, as at the front, the tube's hull was about five meters thick. Unlike the front, however, a round opening perhaps two meters in diameter broke the perfection of the steel plates.

It was rotating toward her. Inside the opening she could just see a light—Dawson must have pulled his torch from his belt to examine the interior.

As the opening neared, she maneuvered closer and, as it passed, grabbed a small round projection set next to it. To avoid getting her shoulder wrenched out of her socket, she fired her spacesuit's thrusters to match the tube's spin as best she could.

After a moment's disorientation, when up and down suddenly flipped, she found herself spinning with the tube. *Voyager* slowly turned above her.

She gazed down the little corridor. Dawson, standing, faced an airlock almost exactly like the one on the little engineering spaceship she'd examined in docking bay two.

She felt her heart begin to hammer. This was it. It had to be. She took back half of what she'd thought about the Sperians. Having the control room on one of the ends made perfect sense.

"Ensign Wong," she said, "join us inside when the opening reaches your position. Take care to match the tube's rotation."

"Yes, sir," she said.

"Dawson, do you see those three small holes set into the bulkhead ahead of you?" she asked, walking forward slowly. The tube's centrifugal force provided the equivalent of gravity, but it was about a third of Earth normal. She had to keep touching the walls and ceiling to keep from bounding too far in any direction.

"Uh—yes," Dawson said.

"Put your fingers in them and turn counterclockwise." It seemed a fair assumption that it worked the same way as the airlock on the little engineering ship.

Dawson twisted a bit; then she heard him grunt. "Got it! It's moving!"

A pale gray light suddenly flooded the little corridor. Light panels on the walls to either side flickered to life. A round hatch swung open ahead of Dawson.

He glanced back. "Shall I . . . ?"

"Right behind you," B'Elanna said.

He stepped through. Suddenly B'Elanna heard a muffled "oof" followed by a grunt.

"What's wrong?" she demanded, hurrying forward to see. He'd vanished from her line of sight. If anything had happened to him, she'd blame herself for not going first. "Dawson—"

"I'm okay," he said suddenly, sounding embarrassed. She saw him stand a little unsteadily. "I tripped over my own feet. Artificial gravity's on in here and I wasn't ready for it."

Relief flooded through her. "Any signs of life?" she asked, reaching the hatch. It led into a small room about three meters deep and two meters wide: the airlock.

"Not a peep," he said. "I don't think anyone's here."

B'Elanna nodded. *Makes sense,* she thought. If there'd been anyone inside, the lights would have been on.

The second she stepped through the hatch into the

airlock, she felt herself starting to fall. She grabbed the hatch's frame for support; Dawson stepped forward and took her arm. Artificial gravity, she thought, just like he'd said. It felt like about three-quarters Earth normal.

After a wave of dizziness passed and her inner ear adjusted to the change, she stood back to give Ensign Wong room to join them. Both she and Dawson grabbed Li's arms and steadied her until she got her feet set.

"I'm okay," the ensign said, straightening.

B'Elanna moved to the far end of the airlock, where another small control panel had been built into the bulkhead. Its lights glowed amber.

"This is exactly like the one on the Sperian's ship," she said. She inserted three fingers and turned counterclockwise. The hatch behind them swung closed, then air began to hiss into the room. When the control panel's lights switched from amber to pale blue, a round hatch leading deeper into the tube opened before them.

B'Elanna ducked through into what had to be the control room they'd been searching for. Strange pieces of machinery, most round and silver-colored, packed every available centimeter of wall and ceiling space. She couldn't see enough through the limited field of vision her helmet offered, so she checked the environmental readouts inside her suit. Twelve degrees: a bit on the cold side. The air pressure was also a little low, but it could sustain life, and the oxygen content was sufficient. She unlatched her helmet and slipped it over her head. Her ears popped; her breath misted the air before her.

Then the smell hit her like a blow: the reek of sweat and machine oil and bodily odors, just like on the Sperian's ship, but a hundred times worse. It was like this on every space station and every space ship before the final environmental controls were in place, she knew. The filters and purification systems were always among the last installed. Engineers grew used to it in time; it was part of the job. Unfortunately, it wasn't part of hers.

Dawson and Wong were watching at her. "It's breathable," she announced. "Save your suits' air."

They quickly removed their helmets.

"What's that smell?" Dawson gasped, blanching.

"No air filters," she said. "Take shallow breaths through your mouth until you get used to it."

She moved forward, unclipping a tricorder from her belt. As she walked, she took readings of the equipment. If there were gauges or any sort of readouts, she didn't see them. She shook her head. Not only did Sperian engineering methods leave something to be desired, she thought, so did their construction and design. It was going to take hours to figure out how the tube worked. All the identical silver spheres made an incredibly confusing jumble.

The only thing that stood out was a small black box near the back wall; it seemed to have been added last, since part of the bulkhead behind it had been sloppily cut away with laser torches. The box's power relays tapped directly into the energy couplings in the wall.

"Begin tracing all the circuits," she told Dawson and Wong. "Start with that black box. I'll let *Voyager* know what we've found."

She picked up her helmet and put it back on.

Finding the control room was an important step to getting the situation under control, she realized, but it wasn't going to be a quick fix. It might take them several days to get everything sorted out. Meanwhile, the captain had to know what they'd found.

With the helmet in place, she nudged the comm bar with her chin, switching to *Voyager*'s channel. Static roared in her ears.

"Torres to *Voyager*," she said over it.

"B'Elanna!" Harry Kim's voice sounded tinny and distant "I've been trying—" Static drowned him out for a second. "—you all right—" More static filled B'Elanna's ears.

"There's too much static!" she said. She glanced at the chronometer. Eight minutes left before the energy discharge: enough time to make her report and get back inside before the blast. "I'll give you a full report in a minute," she said. "Wait till I get clear of the interference."

"—wait okay—" she heard through static.

She pulled off the helmet. "There's too much interference in here," she told Wong and Dawson. "I'm going to have to go outside to talk to *Voyager*."

"Can you take a look at this first, sir?" Dawson asked. He handed her his tricorder.

B'Elanna glanced over the schematic he'd traced from the black box's circuit. *That's odd*, she thought, frowning. Not only did it seem to be a receiver of some kind, its controls led to every other equipment cluster in the room. Realization of what it was slowly dawned on her.

"It's a slave control," she breathed. The tube was being controlled remotely by someone outside.

"And it's receiving signals right now," Wong said urgently.

"Don't touch it," B'Elanna said quickly. "We don't want them to know we've found it yet."

She put her helmet back on and headed for the airlock on the double. *Voyager* had to be warned. Quickly she stepped through, put three fingers into the holes, turned the locking mechanism clockwise, and began to cycle through.

Her thoughts raced ahead. There was only one reason for that black box to be there, she thought: *sabotage*. But who had installed it? Why was it receiving signals—and where were those signals coming from?

Maybe the Sperian aboard *Voyager* did it, she thought. Maybe that's why he escaped when none of the others had. But then she dismissed that theory; it didn't make sense. Why would the Sperian have sent a distress call if he'd caused the damage in the first place? And for that matter why would the box still be receiving signals? No, there was someone else out there, someone who was watching and waiting.

The lights turned from blue to amber; the front hatch popped open. She stepped forward.

Only one thing was certain, she thought: the disaster hadn't been an accident. Someone had deliberately destroyed the Sperians' space city, murdering all those people. And that someone was still out there, still in contact with the tube, still directing its actions.

She climbed out onto the tube's hull, holding on to the projection she'd caught earlier. She felt lightheaded as the galaxy spun around her.

"Torres to *Voyager*," she said.

"B'Elanna!" he said. His transmission suddenly sounded clear again. "Are you all right?"

"Yes," she began. "We've made a discovery—"

She broke off. Sudden movement where there shouldn't have been movement had caught her eye.

She turned toward the white dwarf. Three huge spherical ships, heading straight toward *Voyager* at high speed, were emerging from the star's bright corona.

It's an ambush!

"Sound red alert!" she said urgently. "Raise the shields, Harry! It's a sneak attack! Harry? *Harry?*"

There was no response.

Then the lead ship opened fire.

CHAPTER

10

KATHRYN JANEWAY YAWNED AS SHE STRETCHED THE kinks from her back: unwinding after a long day had never been easy for her, she reflected. Years before, when she'd received her promotion to captain and command of her first ship, her commanding officer had first congratulated her—and then offered his condolences. She hadn't understood it then, but now she did: the never-ending responsibility, the long hours, the stress and strains of daily command, it all bore down upon you until you thought you'd run screaming into the night.

Everyone had a different way of coping with it. Chakotay had tasted such responsibility as head of a Maquis ship; now he fell back on Native American rituals and an animal spirit-guide. Other captains she knew used yoga meditations, strenuous physical exer-

97

cise, or highly focused hobbies or outside interests to keep them sane. She had her holonovels. She set aside half an hour for them every time she felt the stress getting too great, and she'd certainly felt stress today.

She'd left off in the middle of *Wuthering Heights*. The bleak moors had been especially well done, she thought as she settled down in her chair. She closed her eyes for a second, slowing her breathing, getting ready to plunge into Heathcliff's world.

Then the intercom hailed her. "Sickbay to Captain Janeway," she heard the doctor say.

She tapped her badge. "Janeway here. What is it, Doctor?"

"Tuvok attempted a mind-meld with the Sperian," he said. "Unfortunately, there appear to have been side effects."

Janeway felt a jolt of panic run through her. She never should have suggested it, she thought, fearing the worst.

"What sort of side effects?" she asked in a hoarse voice.

"They both woke up, but they appeared to still be telepathically joined. They attempted to leave sickbay together. I had to drug Tuvok. Both he and the Sperian are unconscious at the moment."

"Will there be any permanent damage?" she asked.

"I do not believe so. In fact, they may both wake up within the hour. Both are showing healthy levels of mental activity."

Janeway allowed herself to relax. *The gamble may well have paid off,* she thought.

"Keep me up to date," she said.

"As you wish, Captain. Sickbay out."

Then red alert sounded.

Janeway leaped to her feet, suddenly alert again. This day was turning into an emotional roller-coaster ride, she thought.

"Captain to the bridge," she heard Chakotay's voice say.

She tapped her badge again. "Janeway here. What's wrong?"

"Three warships have appeared," Chakotay said.

"They're not responding to our hails, and they're firing on us. Their first salvo missed. They are preparing to fire again. I've raised shields."

"Take defensive actions. I'm on my way. Janeway out!"

She dashed out the door and headed for the turbolift at a run, but before she'd made it more than halfway, a powerful series of explosions rocked *Voyager*. She careened from bulkhead to bulkhead and almost fell. A second later another explosion shook the ship, and then a secondary alarm klaxon began to sound, one that she'd always dreaded: hull breach. She stopped and listened, but couldn't hear the telltale hiss of escaping air under the blare of the alarms. It had to be another deck.

Voyager lurched underfoot and she heard the engines begin to whine in protest. They were on the verge of overload, she realized. What was Chakotay doing with her ship?

Safety mechanisms suddenly shut down the warp coils, and then the lights went out. Emergency panels lit one by one along the floor: running lights from batteries. This definitely wasn't good, she thought. There had to be major damage to Engineering.

Another explosion shook the *Voyager*. The deck underfoot suddenly canted to the left and an extra gee or two of weight slammed her painfully into the bulkhead. She slumped to the floor, feeling stunned. The inertial dampers weren't able to compensate for whatever Chakotay and Tom Paris were doing, she realized. She had to get to the bridge. She had to know what was going on.

She slapped her badge. "Janeway to Kim!" she yelled. He was the bridge officer least likely to be in the middle of something critical at this point. "Status!"

Harry Kim answered, his voice so calm and smooth she knew he must be scared nearly out of his wits. "Hull breach, deck nineteen, Captain. Warp engines off-line. We're heading into the red giant on full impulse power."

"I'll be there as soon as I can. Keep me informed of anything important. Janeway out."

Thank goodness for Academy stress training, she thought, and thank goodness for the Maquis's battle experience. A lesser crew would be panicking right now. *He said we were heading into the red giant.* It had to be another trick of Chakotay's, she thought. Starfleet manuals didn't cover maneuvers like that. She struggled to her feet and staggered toward the turbolift. She only hoped his trick worked.

Chakotay stood braced against the deck rail, powerful muscles straining to hold himself upright. According to the instruments, they were running at something over two and a half standard Earth gravities. He couldn't be sure any of the readings were accurate, though; half the instrument panels were dead, including the starboard sensor readouts. The inertial dampers weren't able to keep up.

Slowly the weight pulling at him eased. *Now I know why Starfleet has so many backup systems,* he thought wryly. Without them they'd be sitting dead in space right now.

"They're dropping back," Tom Paris said calmly. "Hull temperature approaching critical."

"Realign the thrusters," he said. "Twenty-two degrees."

"Already done, sir," Tom said. "Firing . . . now!"

Gravity seemed to double again. Chakotay braced himself and stared up at the fiery mass of the red giant looming before them. If this didn't work, they'd be dead, fried to atoms in seconds. He'd never liked flying by the seat of his pants, but he'd done it more often than not as part of the Maquis. And this particular trick had worked more than once for him.

But his ship at the time had all its instruments working, and it hadn't massed half as much as *Voyager.* Too late to worry about it, though—either they'd make it, or it wouldn't matter one way or another.

"It's not working!" Tom called. "We're not breaking free!"

"Fire the maneuvering thrusters, too!" Chakotay said, keeping his voice deliberately confident. *Come on,* he thought, pushing on the railing as though he could move the ship by his own sheer physical strength. *Come on, you can make it.*

Tom fired the maneuvering thrusters. The whole ship seemed to shudder. Chakotay felt a fierce escape as an iron wall slammed into him. He braced himself as best he could, but couldn't hold on: he crumpled to the deck. Something in his left arm broke with a sharp *crack!*, and then a wave of pain like a series of white-hot needles pushing into his shoulder swept over him. He heard himself begin to scream—

As a heavy thrumming vibration rose through the deck underneath her and twice her weight tugged at every fiber of her body, Kathryn Janeway pulled herself on by sheer force of will. Fighting to stand erect, she forced herself into the turbolift. I'm the captain, she kept thinking. I have to be on the bridge. That's my place.

Thankfully the turbolift was still running. She climbed inside, clung to the railing, and said, "Bridge!"

Whining in protest, it moved, which was all she needed. The extra gees eased; she began to breathe more easily. At least the explosions had stopped, she thought. Chakotay must have pulled another rabbit out of his Maquis hat.

Gasping, waiting for the doors to open, she wasn't prepared when the ship lurched again and the force of four or five gravities suddenly slammed into her. She felt a moment of weightlessness as the turbolift plunged downward, but it didn't go far—and that gave her enough time to slide down onto her back. It wasn't an acceleration couch, but it would have to do.

As the turbolift slowed and began its inexorable climb up toward the bridge once more, she felt her cheeks pull back and her eyes press almost shut. The extra weight pinned her to the floor. It felt like a ton of bricks piled on her chest and legs and arms. She couldn't move, could barely breathe—

And just as rapidly as the extra weight hit, it let up. Cautiously she climbed to her feet. She felt like one bruise from head to foot, and when she touched her nose, she found she had a nosebleed. No time for that now, though. As if on cue, the turbolift doors opened, and she stepped into what she considered a starship captain's worst nightmare.

Most of the bridge crew lay on the floor moaning or unconscious, including Chakotay. More than half of the instrument readouts showed static or nothing at all. Only two officers still manned their stations: Tom Paris and, a bit to her surprise, Harry Kim. The youngest and the strongest, she thought.

Chakotay tried to pull himself to a sitting position. His left arm had an extra bend and hung at an odd angle, she saw, and he had blood on his face and shirt. "Don't get up, Commander," she said, striding forward. She couldn't worry about him or the others at the moment, thought. First came the ship, then the individuals aboard. "Status report, Mr. Paris," she said.

"We took three direct hits," Tom said. "Decks nineteen and fourteen have hull breaches. Warp engines are off-line. Life support has been restored."

"Engineering just took impulse power off-line," Harry said. "We're down to maneuvering thrusters. We should have seventy percent power to the shields within thirty seconds, plus fifty percent to the phaser banks."

"And we still have photon torpedoes, Captain," Tom said.

"Arm the photon torpedoes," she said. "What's our position relative to our attackers?"

"We used the red giant's gravitational pull to slingshot out of their line of fire," Tom said. "Unfortunately, we didn't have time to factor in the white dwarf's gravitational pull. We're now twenty million kilometers on the other side of the tube."

"The three ships are closing on us once more," Harry said. "At their current speed, they will be in attack range within two and a half minutes."

"It seems we only gained a little time," Janeway said. She drew a deep breath, then sat in the captain's chair.

"Route all auxiliary power to the shields," she said. "Bring us about, Mr. Paris. Prepare to fire photon torpedoes."

She stared at the closing ships on the forward viewscreen. They drew near the tube, passed it, then suddenly veered to the side, away from the *Voyager*. It seemed a odd detour, Janeway thought, narrowing her eyes in thought . . . almost as if they wanted to bring their attack in from a new direction . . . one where no stray shots might hit the tube.

They were trying to protect it, she concluded. It meant something to them. They cared if it was destroyed . . . and that might just be their weakness.

"Impulse power back on-line!" Harry said.

"Mr. Paris, lay in a course for the tube. Take us across its front end. Go! Mr. Kim, route as much power to the starboard deflector shields as you can."

"Got it!" Tom said with a grin. He locked in their course. *Voyager* accelerated smoothly.

"Captain," Harry said, sounding a little alarmed, "the tube is scheduled to fire again in forty-one seconds!"

"That's right, Mr. Kim," she said. She watched the three ships change course once again—this time to intercept *Voyager*.

We're going to make it, she thought.

"They're firing!" Tom said. "We have ninety-three percent power to the starboard shields. This salvo won't make it through."

A huge bolt of energy had appeared from the lead ship. It shimmered, growing steadily larger. Janeway braced herself for impact, counting down the seconds. Three . . . two . . . one . . .

The whole ship jolted, but the shields seemed to hold.

A whining noise started somewhere in the impulse engines. How long till the tube fired? It couldn't be long, she thought. Twenty seconds? Twenty-five?

"No damage," Tom said. "Shields holding at sixty-seven percent."

"Will we make it across?" she asked. "We're cutting it close."

He studied his readouts. "Yes—with four seconds to spare," he said.

She stood. "Hail the lead ship," she said.

"They're still not responding," Harry said.

"Make it an open broadcast."

"Aye, Captain. Ready."

She took a deep breath. "This is Captain Kathryn

Janeway of the Federation starship *Voyager*. I wish to speak to the commander of the three vessels in pursuit of my ship."

"No reply," Harry said.

Janeway frowned, but went on, "I realize how this situation must appear to you. Nevertheless, you have my assurance that we had nothing to do with the destruction in this system. We are here in response to a distress call, and we have taken one survivor aboard. He is now in our sickbay."

"Still no response," Harry said.

"End transmission," she said. She returned to her seat. Only a few more seconds, she thought, watching the chronometer tick them off.

"How far back are they?" she asked suddenly.

"Six thousand kilometers and closing fast," Tom said.

The mouth of the tube suddenly yawned before them. Energy pulsed inside, a hellish red glow. She found herself holding her breath. If they'd miscalculated by even a few seconds—

Then they flashed past, and a heartbeat later a brilliant white light filled the bridge as the tube fired its mammoth charge of energy.

And half a second later the first shock wave hit.

CHAPTER 11

B'ELANNA HAD WATCHED WITH MINGLED HORROR AND anger as the attack unfolded above her. The three round silver ships fired as one, launching a devastating barrage of what looked like photon torpedoes and bolts of electromagnetic energy. Above her, *Voyager* shook noticeably as first one, then another, then another blast hit. Flames shot out of a hole that suddenly appeared in the hull.

A low moan escaped her. "Run!" she cried. "Get out of here! Don't wait for the next hit!"

As if in response, *Voyager* began to turn. The nacelles began to power up for warp acceleration, then abruptly failed. On impulse power alone, *Voyager* limped off toward the red giant.

The three ships turned in pursuit. The lead ship

fired again, but *Voyager* veered sharply and the blasts narrowly missed. Shields seemed to be failing or down altogether, B'Elanna thought. And there wasn't a thing she could do to help.

Again *Voyager* turned, this time heading straight for the red giant. The three ships followed, laying down another fierce barrage of shots. Several more struck—at least one piercing the hull. There were just too many of them attacking, she thought angrily. She felt a stirring in her blood and longed to be up there with her friends, fighting to survive.

The battle wasn't over yet, though, if she knew Commander Chakotay. Why did she have to be here, where she couldn't help? *Or maybe I can help,* she thought suddenly.

She remembered the firepower of the tube. If she could figure out the controls, swing it around, and use it herself—

She turned and hurried back inside. She had a lot of work to do, she thought. Quickly she twisted the airlock's controls. The hatch shut and air began to fill the chamber. Seven minutes. You could work miracles in seven minutes, she thought. She was going to have to.

As soon as the air pressure rose enough to support life, she slipped off her helmet and cycled through the airlock. Dawson and Wong barely glanced up from their tricorders.

"Don't stop work," she said, then briefed them as she pulled out her own tricorder and began frantically searching for the control mechanism. The two ensigns paled, and she noticed Li's hands shaking a bit, but they kept at their tasks with renewed energy.

The minutes ticked away. Five minutes, four. B'Elanna found the thruster controls and gave a small cry of triumph, but then she realized she had no way to take aim.

Three minutes.

They weren't going to make it, she knew deep inside. She began to despair. Even if she found the aiming controls now, she realized, *Voyager* had been heading toward the red giant. With the tube's little thrusters, it would take half an hour to turn that far around. It was hopeless.

Sighing, she paused and looked up, toward the last place she'd seen *Voyager*. One minute left. Sixty seconds could be an eternity in space, she knew. *Voyager* could already be a drifting, burnt-out, lifeless hulk.

She couldn't go back outside, not with the tube about to fire. She'd just have to wait . . . and pray.

Not knowing, though—that was the worst part.

Neelix had been in his cabin working on the power supply from the Sperian bulkhead before red alert first sounded. The power supply lay in pieces before him. It was a pretty generic unit, he thought, manufactured by the Thalusian Enclave for export throughout this quadrant. It had a variety of settings so it could be used by many different races with many different technological levels and needs. It wouldn't be hard to change its modulation to match Starfleet specifications . . . it was just a matter of adjusting a few switches *here, here,* and *here.*

He smiled and snapped the front panel back in place. Done! Easy enough, and sure to make Paul

Fairman happy. He'd just let him know he could pick it up, and that would be that.

He tapped his badge.

The second he touched it, an alarm klaxon blared and red alert lights flashed. "Off! Sorry! Oh! Sorry!" he said. He slapped the badge. "Off! Sorry! Off!"

The red alert didn't switch off, nor did the alarm klaxon. He realized then that tapping his comm badge hadn't turned them on in the first place. Something was very, very wrong.

"Battle stations!" Harry Kim's voice came over the intercom. "We're under attack!"

Attack? Neelix yelped in panic. What had Janeway and these crazy humans gotten him into now? An explosion suddenly rocked the ship. Neelix dove and barely caught the power supply in time as it slid toward the edge of the table.

"No you don't," he said. "I worked too hard to get you."

The deck canted underfoot. He staggered toward the far wall and steadied himself against the bed. Another explosion rocked the ship; then he felt *Voyager* start to accelerate. *That's it,* he mentally cheered. *Get us out of the way of danger.*

As the force of several gravities crashed into him, he let himself fall on the bed. Better here than on the floor, he thought. He just hoped nothing serious had gone wrong. He didn't like the sound of those explosions—or of the tinny second alarm that had just begun to ring.

What about Kes—she'd been in sickbay, he realized. If anything happened to her, he didn't know what he'd do.

* * *

When red alert sounded, the doctor reacted instantly. The power systems were down, so he opened a panel in the side of the diagnostic table and brought out restraints, which he fitted loosely around Tuvok's arms and legs.

"Why are you doing that?" Kes asked.

"In case things get bumpy," he said, "we have to make sure he doesn't fall off the table and do himself more harm. Take care of the Sperian."

The deck suddenly jolted underfoot, almost throwing Kes to the floor. "I see what you mean," she said, regaining her balance. She took the Sperian's arm and fastened it exactly the way the doctor was doing with Mr. Tuvok. Then she felt *Voyager* accelerate, and suddenly she felt twice normal gravity bearing down on her.

"Inertial dampers appear to be failing," the doctor said. A second alarm began to ring; then the deck lurched again. Kes didn't like the sound of it. She had a feeling something very, very wrong had happened.

The doctor didn't hesitate. The second he finished with Tuvok, he picked her up and carried her to the next diagnostic table, where he laid her down.

She could barely move her head to look at him. She felt like she weighed a ton.

"What about you—" she began.

He shook his head. "I'm a hologram, remember? Light isn't affected by acceleration as much as flesh and blood is." He began strapping her down. "Try to breathe normally. The second alarm means there's a hull breach, but I don't believe it's on this deck. Sickbay has its own air supply, however, and if necessary we'll switch to that."

Kes began to grow concerned. This sounded quite serious. "Neelix—" she began. If anything happened to him, she didn't know what she'd do.

"Mr. Neelix is more than capable of looking after himself," the doctor said. "For the moment, you and our two patients are my only concerns."

CHAPTER

12

MY LUCK HAS NEVER BEEN WORSE, PAUL FAIRMAN thought bitterly. He clenched his fists and tried not to scream. It wasn't so much the pressure, like an elephant on his chest, or the pain from being slammed to the floor at three gravities and hearing something in his left knee pop like a wine cork.

What hurt most was being trapped on this accursed ship in the middle of nowhere. He hadn't signed on with the Maquis to traipse around the Delta Quadrant as part of a Federation crew. If he'd wanted that, he would have tried to join Starfleet Academy in the first place.

Instead, he'd drifted around the civilized part of the galaxy, doing odd jobs, running little scams, smuggling alien artifacts or exotic alcoholic beverages or whatever else paid the most that particular week.

He'd learned the hard way that the only person you could depend on was yourself. That was the problem with being an orphan, he thought; you couldn't even fall back on your family for help.

And now Janeway seemed to be trying to kill him, along with the rest of the crew. He didn't like it one bit.

We should've just kept on going, he thought bitterly, and not for the first time. *Voyager shouldn't stop for anyone or anything till we get home. That's the only way we're going to make it. Otherwise we'll be mapping this sector for the rest of our lives.*

The Starfleet crew might like that. The Maquis crew might accept it. But not Paul Fairman. He had bigger plans.

In all his dealings on half a hundred planets, he had noticed one universal. Whether Klingon or human or Vulcan or Romulan, everyone wanted food the way Mother used to make it.

Of course, "Mother" might be a green-and-blue slug or an emotionless calculating machine like a Vulcan. But that really didn't matter. The principle worked, and it worked well. The last two years of his life back home, he'd made his way selling replicator technology to worlds without it. Of course, that violated the Prime Directive half the time, but he'd always thought the Prime Directive so much nonsense anyway. Wasn't it better to feed the hungry, end starvation, and make quite a bit of money in the process?

If only the Federation hadn't blasted his ship to so much scrap metal while trying to stifle free trade, he would've had it made by now. If only the Federation hadn't found and confiscated his private cache of gold-pressed latinum, he could've bought himself a new planet-hopper. And if only he hadn't had to join the Maquis to get off that hellhole of a world, New Russia, he'd be safe in human space right now. . . .

He smiled fatalistically to himself. He'd always been a survivor. He rolled with every punch the galaxy threw at him, then came back stronger than ever. What worked in the past kept on working.

He had a plan that would guarantee him a place of respect among the crew. There wouldn't be much money in it, but there would certainly be influence, and out here, with nothing to buy, that might be all he needed.

He felt the weight on his chest lessen. When he tried to move his legs, lancets of white-hot pain shot through the whole left side of his body. He gasped, then lay still.

The engines were making a horrible sound. He felt a pounding vibration through the deck beneath him.

A hull-breach alarm had begun to ring.

We're not going to make it, he thought with despair.

The tube fired and kept on firing.

Kathryn Janeway sat out the resulting shock waves in silence, watching and waiting for the three ships to reappear, circling around the energy beam. When they didn't, she took a deep breath and let it out slowly. Hadn't she left them with enough time to steer clear? Any cadet at the Academy could have run rings around that beam of energy. She had hoped the shock waves from the subspace distortion might incapacitate their ships or at the very least buy them more time. But had she miscalculated? Had she inadvertently sent them to their deaths? The thought alarmed and disturbed her.

Even though they'd been attacking the *Voyager*, it had been a misunderstanding, one that could easily have been cleared up. Now she could only hope, somehow, that they'd survived. Everything could so easily have been cleared up if they'd given her a chance to talk.

She'd worry about them later, she decided. For now, they had their own problems to worry about . . . like the hull breaches and the failed warp engines . . . like her crew.

She rose and crossed to Chakotay, who was now sitting up and cradling his left arm in his lap. His face looked ashen and his lips had turned a pale blue. Around him, the rest of the downed bridge officers were also moaning and stirring, but none looked as bad as he did.

"How are you?" she asked, kneeling.

"Broken arm," he said with a grimace.

"You saved the ship."

"I got caught with my pants down." He grabbed the railing and struggled to pull himself up. Janeway got her shoulder under his good arm and helped. "They used a Maquis trick, coming out of the white dwarf's corona."

"Report to sickbay," she said. She turned to Tom Paris. "Mr. Paris, you can put that field-medic training to use now. See Chakotay to sickbay, then do what you can do to assist Kes and the doctor." She had a feeling they would be getting overwhelmed right about now.

"Right, Captain." He stood a little uncertainly. "But—"

Janeway slid behind his console. "Don't worry, Mr. Paris. I'm quite capable of keeping your seat warm until another pilot gets here. I have flown before, you know."

"Yes, Captain." He took Chakotay's good arm and helped him to the turbolift, which opened as if everything were normal. *At least something's still working,* Janeway thought.

She turned to Harry Kim. "Get someone up here to take over for Mr. Paris," she said. "I want a full list of officers and crew still on their feet. You have five minutes."

"Yes, Captain."

She turned and gazed out toward where the three Sperian ships had been before the shock wave. The tube had finally stopped firing. Now she could find out what had happened to them. She prayed they hadn't been vaporized.

She hesitated a moment, then activated the thrusters, moving them forward at an eighth impulse power.

She glanced over at Harry. "Can you locate their ships?" she asked. "Are they . . . ?"

"I have them on my sensors now," he said slowly. "The lead ship is drifting. So are the other two. . . . One has life support operational. The other two appear to be completely powerless." He looked up. "Apparently they don't believe in backup systems. They seem to be completely knocked out."

"Save your congratulations," she said. "We still

have plenty of problems of our own. I want a damage report from Engineering."

"That's coming in now," Harry said. "Engineering reports warp drive out for twenty-two hours. We have substantial damage to decks eight, twelve, fourteen, and nineteen, including two hull breaches which are now being patched. Transporters are out for at least six hours. They're also going to have to shut down impulse power to lock off a radiation leak on deck three."

"Can you reach Lieutenant Torres?" she asked. "I'd like her here to supervise repairs."

"I'll try." He turned back to his console. "She's not responding," he said a moment later, then added, "I had trouble reaching her before the attack. There appears to be interference from the tube."

"Keep trying," she said.

Now, B'Elanna Torres thought, ending her mental countdown toward the start of the tube's blast. She held her breath expectantly.

Nothing happened. She listened for several heartbeats, but nothing seemed out of the ordinary. Perhaps it didn't go off, she thought.

She turned to Dawson. "I don't—"

A deafening roar drowned out her words. The lights in the control panel dimmed to the faintest of glows and the deck underfoot began to vibrate. She looked down. At first it felt like a light tremor; then it began to shake harder and harder until it pounded through the soles of her feet and made her teeth rattle.

"Helmets on!" she cried.

Dawson and Wong stared at her. Wong called

something, but B'Elanna couldn't hear a word through the tidal wave of sound rushing over them.

She picked up her helmet and snapped it into place, motioning for both ensigns to follow suit. They did so. When she dogged the helmet's latches securely, she could still hear the roar of the beam outside, but it sounded far away, like a distant waterfall. *Much better.*

She nudged the comm bar with her chin. "Dawson, keep monitoring that black box. If you can find a way to tap into it, I want to know what information it's receiving and transmitting."

"Yes, sir," he said, turning to the task.

"Wong," she said, "I've found the thruster controls—this whole assembly here—but I haven't been able to spot any guidance mechanism. Check the rear station while I check the front. I want to be able to turn this tube around next time it's ready to fire." *If only Voyager can hold on that long,* B'Elanna thought.

"Yes, Lieutenant," Li Wong said. She headed for the back of the control room.

B'Elanna took a deep breath. She usually found the recycled air in a spacesuit metallic and stifling, but after the stench of the Sperian control room, it was almost a joy. Raising her tricorder, she began tracing the next circuit.

For a second she thought she'd found the guidance system, but then it turned out to be a warp field capacitor . . . or possibly a warp field transducer. The intricacies of the design began to fill her mind. What was this machine *really* designed to do?

She almost missed it when the vibration faded and complete silence returned to the control room.

"Voyager to—" she suddenly heard Harry Kim saying over a wild hiss of static. *"Voyager* to Torres."

More static drowned him out.

"Torres here," she replied, the words catching in her throat. *Voyager* was still out there. They hadn't been destroyed. She grinned suddenly. *It's just like Chakotay to pull a rabbit out of his hat.*

"Voyager to—" she heard Harry begin again, then more static obliterated his voice. He clearly hadn't heard her.

"Kim, this is Torres," she repeated. "I'm heading outside. Hold on."

He didn't answer. *At least he's alive,* she thought jubilantly, and that was enough. "I'll be right back," she said to Dawson and Wong, starting for the airlock.

CHAPTER

13

WHEN TUVOK OPENED HIS EYES, HE HAD THE STRANGEST feeling of loss. Something unsettling had happened during the mind-meld, he thought.

He levered himself up on his elbows and shook his head, trying to clear it. The doctor had injected him with something, he recalled. Its aftereffects left him giddy and disoriented and slightly nauseated. When he swallowed, his tongue felt thick and fuzzy; a faint metallic taste lingered in the back of his mouth.

Tetramyzol. He recognized the symptoms. It was a mild sedative derived from night-blooming sponges in the caves below the dry seas of Vulcan. It temporarily lowered brain-wave activity and induced sleep when administered properly. The doctor seemed to have done so.

He sat all the way up. He had been lying on one of

the biotables in sickbay, he saw, and considerable time appeared to have passed. Dozens of patients filled the room, and Chakotay was lying on a biobed opposite him. Kes was doing something to his arm.

"Hello, Mr. Tuvok," he heard Tom Paris say behind him. "Glad to see you're awake. We sure could have used you on the bridge."

Tuvok turned his head. Friend Tom had come up behind him. He was holding a glass of what looked like a pinkish yellow juice.

"Is that for me?" Tuvok asked. His tongue felt thick; his voice rasped strangely when he spoke.

"Yeah." Friend Tom passed it over, and Tuvok sipped gently. It was guava and *psaat*-fruit juice, he found: a little tart but it quenched his thirst. "The doctor said you'd want it when you woke up," Friend Tom went on. "Something about electrolytes?"

Tuvok swung his legs around to the floor and finished the juice in two long swallows. Once more his body had begun to respond to his will, he found. The nausea passed and his thoughts seemed significantly clearer.

"What happened?" he asked. "Why are there so many injured people in sickbay?"

"We had a running battle with three Sperian warships," Friend Tom said. "But don't worry, they're knocked out for the moment."

"How long have I been unconscious?" Tuvok asked.

"I don't know—at least half an hour. That's how long I've been down here helping out. How do you feel?"

Tuvok considered the question. "I feel—indescribably strange," he finally said. "As though a large part of me is missing."

"Missing?" Friend Tom said, his brow creasing. "What do you mean?"

"I am not quite sure," Tuvok said. Indeed, he found the thought puzzling; he would have to consider it again at a more opportune moment. "I do not recall ever experiencing this sensation after initiating a mind-meld."

"I think I have the answer," Friend Doctor said, joining them. He raised a medical tricorder and began scanning Tuvok.

"I would like to hear it," Tuvok said. He leaned forward slightly to see the medical tricorder's readouts, but the doctor tilted the display panel back.

"Like Vulcans," Friend Doctor said, "Sperians have copper-based blood. About an hour before your mind-meld, I tried to awaken our guest with a Vulcan stimulant—tetsorum D."

"Of course," Tuvok said, nodding. That might well explain the odd effects of the mind-meld.

"I don't follow you," Friend Tom said.

"Tetsorum D is a psychotrope," Tuvok said, "and psychotropes stimulate mental abilities, including telepathy and empathy. I suspect Sozoas has latent telepathic abilities which the drug brought to the fore." He stood, straightening his uniform with precise grace. Now that his body had recovered sufficiently to return to duty, he had to find the Faction Leader and make his report. He knew it was imperative. Logically, there could be no other action on his part.

"You shouldn't be up," the doctor said. "You look pale, and your electrolyte levels are still low."

"I am sufficiently recovered to resume my duties, Doctor." Tuvok handed his glass back to Friend Tom.

"More, please." He turned to Friend Doctor when Tom went to fetch the juice. "The mind-meld worked too well," he said. "The Sperian and I became a composite being, neither one nor the other but something of each. We had access to both our sets of memories and found a commonality which allowed us to function as if we were a single organism. I believe we experienced something similar to what Trills undergo when they bond with their symbionts."

"That is possible," the doctor admitted. "Starfleet medical documentation on Vulcan mind-melds and possible side effects under psychotropic drugs is not as extensive as it might be."

"The combination is generally avoided. Vulcans consider it dangerous; I would not have attempted the mind-meld had I known Sozoas had been injected with a psychotrope."

"My apologies," the doctor said. "I should have informed you when I discovered your intent."

"Not necessary, Doctor. I appear to have suffered no lasting ill effects." Tuvok accepted another glass of juice from Friend Tom. "What happened to Sozoas?"

"Is that the Sperian's name?" Friend Doctor asked.

"Yes."

"He lapsed back into unconsciousness the moment you released him. However, his brain activity has increased dramatically, so he may awaken soon."

"Did you learn anything from him?" Friend Tom asked.

"I believe so," Tuvok said. He thought about the tube, and details of the Tech Faction's warp-acceleration project came flooding back: how the Faction had funded the project secretly for twelve years while competing with the Military Faction for jurisdiction over it, how this binary star system had been selected for the final working machine, how it achieved operational status only to malfunction. "In fact," he said, "I learned a great deal."

Indeed, all the information he could possibly need now came readily to mind when he thought about it . . . as if he had actually lived through the experiment himself.

He drained his second glass of juice and handed it back to Friend Tom again. "Thank you," he said. Then he bowed to all of them. "If you will excuse me," he went on, "I have to make my report to Leader Janeway."

He strode from sickbay without a backward glance. He was aware of a startled silence behind him and hoped he hadn't offended Friend Doctor or Friend Tom; sometimes non-Vulcan interpersonal interactions confounded him with their illogical ways. Though he tried to maneuver slowly through their emotionally charged world, sometimes it became tricky.

Leader Janeway—?" he heard Friend Tom say just as the doors to sickbay whisked closed behind him.

He tapped his badge on his way to the turbolift. "Tuvok to Janeway."

"Janeway here," she responded instantly.

"I retrieved the information we required," he said. "I wish to make my report. I believe you will find it of interest."

"Join me on the bridge," she said.

For the moment, the situation seemed stable, Janeway thought, which was about the best she could hope for. With Tuvok awake and Chakotay recovering, they'd soon be on top of things.

"I've got Lieutenant Torres now, Captain!" Harry Kim said suddenly.

More good news—it seemed everything was coming together at once. Janeway raised her head and addressed her distant chief engineer: "Lieutenant, *Voyager* has received substantial damage. I need you back aboard to oversee repairs."

The turbolift doors whisked open and Janeway glanced back to see Tuvok stepping onto the bridge. She nodded to him; he looked much his old self, she thought. He crossed to her side, but she held up her hand before he could speak.

"Captain," B'Elanna's voice came in, full of static. "We've found the tube's control room."

"Let it go for now," she said. "We can return to it later." Or the Sperians could take over, she thought. That might be the wisest course, once they established contact.

"You don't understand," B'Elanna said. "The space city's destruction was sabotage. Someone wired a remote sensing device into the controls here. It's still being monitored."

"Still? Do you mean right now?" She bit her lip,

considering the possibilities. Sabotage . . . suddenly things were starting to make sense.

"I believe so," B'Elanna said. "I can check, if you want."

"Do so," Janeway said. "We incapacitated the three ships that came after us. They shouldn't be controlling the tube any more."

"Hold on . . . this is going to take a minute. . . ." Static filled the intercom. Harry Kim quickly lowered the volume.

Janeway turned to Tuvok and filled him in. He listened attentively, but offered no insights of his own.

"What do you make of her discovery, Mr. Tuvok?" she asked when she finished.

"Curious," he said, "that these three ships were not aware of the tube's impending discharge. It would seem to indicate that they were not, in fact, the ones who planted the control device."

"Agreed," she said, turning back to face the monitor. "The real villains are still out there. Did you learn anything from the Sperian?"

"He knew nothing about any sabotage. Indeed, as far as he was concerned, the warp-acceleration tube malfunctioned."

"Warp acceleration tube?" Janeway took a deep breath. That sounded interesting—and also like it shouldn't be discussed on the bridge. "We'll talk about it later, in my ready room," she said.

"Agreed."

"What is your analysis of the situation?"

"Two possibilities present themselves," Tuvok went on. "One is that another ship or group of ships is out there watching us now, either preparing to strike or doing nothing so we will continue to be blamed for the space city's destruction."

"And the other possibility?"

"That another ship or group of ships is only interested in sabotaging the tube and we are—at least for the present—outside the scope of their interest or responsibility."

"I'm not sure I like either possibility," Janeway said.

B'Elanna's voice cut in again. "Captain, the box is still picking up transmissions."

"Can you tell where they're coming from?"

"No," she said. "It's sending out a subspace carrier wave, but it's broadband, not aimed in any one direction."

Janeway nodded slowly; these mysterious saboteurs weren't going to make it easy for her to track them down, it seemed. "Based on what you've found," she said to B'Elanna, "I think your work in the control room must take priority. I want you to stay there and see what else you can find out about it."

"Yes, Captain."

"We will pick up the rest of your team so they can assist on *Voyager*'s repairs. Lieutenant Carey can oversee that operation."

"Do you have transporters up?" B'Elanna asked.

Janeway glanced back at Harry, who shook his head.

"Not yet," she said. "Warp engines and defensive systems are a higher priority."

"I can disable the remote-control box now, if you want," B'Elanna said.

Janeway glanced at Tuvok. "Your recommendation?"

"I recommend against it," he said. "If the saboteurs are for some reason not yet aware of us, we do not want to alert them to our presence."

"At least not in our current state," she agreed. "Leave the box alone," she told B'Elanna. "Do nothing to disturb it. But work on figuring out how to slave control of the tube over here."

"How long until you can pick up my team?" B'Elanna asked.

Janeway laid in the course and accelerated at a quarter impulse power. "I estimate three minutes," she said. *Then we can let Engineering shut down impulse engines*, she thought.

"We'll be ready," B'Elanna promised.

"Any signals from those Sperian ships?" she asked Harry.

"Nothing yet, Captain."

"Keep an ear out for them," she said. She touched her comm badge. "Janeway to sickbay."

"We're still rather busy here right now, Captain," the holographic doctor said, a little archly. She could hear the babble of dozens of voices in the background. "If you're calling about the Sperian, I'm afraid he still hasn't regained consciousness."

"Keep an eye on him, Doctor."

"I will. Sickbay out."

Janeway leaned back. She'd have B'Elanna see if something could be done about the doctor's bedside manner the next time they had downtime, she decided. He had really begun to get on her nerves.

B'Elanna didn't have to completely reprogram him: a tweak here and there to make him a little more politely responsive would do. As it was, she felt like a schoolgirl every time they spoke.

An ensign in red and black appeared at her elbow: Richard N'gara, a pilot from the Maquis crew. Despite his light brown skin, she could see a rapidly purpling bruise on his cheek and another on his forehead, but otherwise he looked uninjured.

"I'm here to relieve this position, Captain," he said in his deep voice.

"Please." She stood, allowing him to slip into the vacant seat. "We're going to pick up two crewmen at the tube, Ensign. Once they're safely aboard, bring us to a stationary position five thousand meters from the three drifting vessels. Hold there facing them."

"Aye, Captain," he said. He began checking the readouts.

The turbolift doors opened; a repair crew from Engineering entered. They went at once to the science station, opened the panel, and began pulling out modular sensor relays and replacing them. Lieutenant Carey seemed to have things well in hand, she thought.

"Any changes in the Sperian ships?" she asked Marta Dvorak.

"Yes, Captain," she said, examining the sensor readout. "I believe the second ship may have life-support functions restored within the hour. All three ships appear to have sustained severe damage from the energy blast as well as the resultant shock waves.

None of them will pose a threat to us for several days."

"Are their crews in any immediate danger?"

"No."

"Good." She rose. "Now, Mr. Tuvok, if you'd be so kind as to join me in my ready room?"

CHAPTER 14

PAUL FAIRMAN WALKED GINGERLY. HE DIDN'T FEEL ANY real pain in his knee anymore—that holographic doctor had done an adequate enough job of patching him up—but he still didn't trust the leg to support his full weight. After all, it wasn't like that hologram was a real flesh-and-blood person; what did he know about suffering? Paul knew; he'd suffered mightily.

Everything would be different when he had that power supply. When would Neelix have it for him? Everyone kept talking about what a great scavenger Neelix was supposed to be—oh, he got the captain this, and he got the galley that—but anyone could have done that much. Hell, a Ferengi could have done all that Neelix had done, plus cut enough deals to own half the Delta Quadrant by now.

When he rounded the corner and almost bumped into the Neelix, he stopped in surprise.

"Just the fellow I'm looking for," Neelix said happily. "I have a power supply that just might work for you."

"What—already?" Amazement flooded through him. He'd been grumbling to himself, but he'd expected to have to wait several weeks or even months, till the next time they made planetfall.

"It's in my cabin," Neelix said.

"Great!" Fairman smiled. Finally things were starting to go his way. It was about time, considering all that he'd gone through.

"There's only one thing," Neelix said.

Of course, there had to be a catch. "What?" he asked suspiciously.

"I want to know how you're going to use it first."

He's a greedy little bugger, just like a Ferengi. Fairman smiled. Perhaps that was a good sign. If he cut Neelix in for a small percentage, it might guarantee his loyalty in the future.

Fairman forced a smile and a laugh. "Well, maybe I can give you a piece of the action." He put an arm around Neelix's shoulder and lowered his voice to a conspiratorial whisper. "It's this way. . . ."

Leader Janeway settled into the chair behind her desk in her ready room, looking at him expectantly. Tuvok stood before her, his legs slightly spread, his arms behind his back: his usual stance when making a report.

He opened his mouth to begin, but she interrupted.

"First," she said, "I want to know how you feel. Are you certain you're up to resuming your duties?"

"I can assure you," he said, "that I am both mentally and physically fit."

She nodded slowly. "Very well, Mr. Tuvok. Your report."

"The tube," he began, "is, in fact, a secret project of the Sperians, as we had surmised. It is not a weapon, however, but the first working model of a highly advanced warp accelerator."

"You mentioned that before. A warp accelerator?" Leader Janeway leaned forward, and he saw her keen interest reflected in her expression. He knew she must be wondering if this device might be able to provide them with a means to return home. "This sounds more and more interesting," she said. "How does it work?"

"Essentially, a ship accelerates to warp speed inside the tube, which simultaneously builds up its own warp field with a reverse polarity. The device should, in theory, produce an effect like shooting a projectile from a gun."

"You said 'in theory.' Explain."

"It didn't work."

"What went wrong? If it was just the sabotage, we can fix that."

"I suspect the entire Sperian design is deeply flawed. We have seen how poorly Sperians build both spaceships and space stations. I have confirmed, from direct contact with Sozoas's mind, that this is a flaw inherent in all of their engineering. To successfully control a warp field of the size and strength generated by their warp accelerator, every element of the device would have to be aligned and calibrated to exacting standards. Where theory may in fact produce working computer simulations, the ability to execute their designs at this scale is lacking."

"But with our equipment and resources . . ." she mused.

Tuvok shook his head. "I believe it is well beyond the technical capabilities of this ship . . . and perhaps of Starfleet itself. Federation scientists experimented with a similar acceleration project thirty-six years ago, but gave it up because the ability to balance such immense forces so exactingly and on such a scale was beyond their ability."

Leader Janeway nodded. "Yes, I have read about that. The Charles Montgomery project. Several ships were destroyed, I believe."

"They imploded while attempting warp acceleration," he said. "Twenty-six experienced officers lost their lives. It was considered a costly disaster and quietly shelved."

"But if the Sperians' project wasn't going to work," Leader Janeway said slowly, returning to the problem at hand, "why bother to sabotage it? Why not wait and watch it fail?"

"Clearly the saboteurs believed it *would* work."

"I don't understand. Neelix said the Sperians don't have any enemies. Are there any likely suspects? The Kazon, perhaps?"

"Unlikely, Captain. The culprits are most likely the Sperians themselves."

"Explain."

"The history of the warp-accelerator project is a long and tumultuous one, and to grasp it you must first have a basic understanding of Sperian society, which is where the roots of the problem lie."

Leader Janeway leaned back. "You have my full attention."

"Essentially, Sperian culture consists of conflicting Factions who form temporary alliances in order to reach goals of mutual interest. It is a vast and confusing bureaucracy. At the moment, there are three Factions which concern us: the Industrial Faction, which oversees the building and maintenance of all space projects; the Military Faction, which oversees defense, exploration, and exploitation of Sperian space; and the Tech Faction, which consists of engineers and scientists. The Tech Faction designed the warp accelerator and, in alliance with the Industrial Faction, oversaw its construction. The Military Faction tried to assume control over the project in its early stages, claiming it fell within their rightful influence, but both the Tech Faction and the Industrial Faction blocked that move, at which time it was submitted to the Council of Factions. After many years of arguments, squabbles, grandstanding, and covert influence peddling, the Tech Faction won out."

"So the Military Faction tried to destroy it."

"It's not as clearly cut as that, unfortunately. Within each Faction are subFactions which share interests with other Factions. You can belong to one or many different subFactions depending on your interests and family ties. Our Sperian refugee, for example, is a member of the Tech Faction while also belonging to the Mining subFaction, the Farmers subFaction, and the Industrial subFaction of his primary Faction. Because of his birth-heritage—his first mother belongs to the Tech Faction—he placed his primary affiliation there. Because his secondary mother belongs to the Farmers Faction, he also belongs to that subFaction, although he takes no active part in its politics. His father belongs to the Mining Faction, which is really a self-governing part of the Industrial Faction, but it gets its own seat on the Central Council of Factions, so—"

"I get the point," Leader Janeway said, breaking in. "My head is starting to spin from all these Factions and subFactions. If this is a taste of how the Sperian culture operates, I can see where Neelix got his horror stories of dealing with their bureaucratic ways."

"Indeed," Tuvok said, "I thought human politics were complicated until I experienced some of what Sozoas has gone through. The Sperians are fully as argumentative, bureaucratic, and obstructionist as Mr. Neelix indicated."

"In short," Leader Janeway said, "we have no way of knowing whether it was the Military Faction or a subFaction of the Tech or Industrial Factions—or an entirely different Faction altogether—who sabotaged their warp-acceleration project."

"Exactly."

"Did you establish our guest's innocence?"

"Yes. He was on his way to the accelerator to check out a strange power buildup when it began to blast the space city. The shock waves threw his vessel clear, but knocked out the navigation systems. I believe the three Tech Faction ships we disabled came in answer to his distress call."

"Interesting," she mused.

Tuvok suddenly stepped forward and leaned

against her desk. He felt dizzy, and the room spun a bit before him. What was wrong? An aftereffect of the mind-meld?

"Tuvok? Tuvok?"

He looked up. Leader Janeway had come around from behind her desk. She looked concerned.

He forced himself upright. "I am just a little dizzy," he said. "Thank you for your concern."

"Maybe you should see the doctor again," she said.

"I think I require food," he said. That seemed a logical request. His electrolytes were probably still a little off.

"See to it, then." Leader Janeway returned to her seat. "I'll call you if anything happens."

CHAPTER 15

AFTER SEEING DAWSON AND WONG SAFELY BACK ABOARD *Voyager*, B'Elanna returned to the tube's control room. She had a lot of work to do here, she thought. Rather than search again for the tube's steering controls, though, she focused her attentions on the small black box.

She knew it was constantly receiving and transmitting signals; the tricorder told her that much. Unfortunately, she had no way to tell where those signals originated from or went to—or even what they said. Not only were the signals encrypted, they had to be in Sperian.

Then inspiration struck. She could have beaten herself in the head with a bar of rhodinium. Logically, as Tuvok would have said, the monitor had to be wired into all the systems she needed to access to control the tube.

It must have been stress, she told herself. How could she have been so blind?

With renewed energy, she returned to tracing the circuits. And as she worked, she began to see a pattern developing. *Devious,* she thought. *Very, very devious.* Perhaps these Sperians were better engineers than she'd given them credit for being.

"Sickbay to Janeway," the doctor said over the intercom.

"Go ahead, Doctor," Janeway said. She sat back and rubbed her eyes. *This had better be good news,* she thought.

"You said you wanted me to keep you informed of any changes. The Sperian is stirring; I believe he will soon regain consciousness."

"Excellent news, Doctor," Janeway said. "How did you do it?"

"It wasn't me," the doctor said, "it was Tuvok's mind-meld. Sozoas has shown steady improvement since he underwent it.

"In fact," he went on, "I believe he'll be awake within the hour."

"Let me know the minute he regains consciousness," Janeway said. "We need to talk to him."

"Acknowledged," the doctor said.

"You have a *what?*" Neelix looked stunned.

"Not so loud!" Paul Fairman whispered. He licked his lips and looked nervously up and down the corridor. They were almost to his cabin. He stepped up to the door and, when it opened, he pulled Neelix inside.

"Did you say—a *replicator?*" Neelix demanded.

"That's right," Fairman said proudly. "A Reflux 2000, the finest replicator ever made. It's a beauty, the cream of the crop, ready to be patched into any power source. And I do mean *any.*"

"Where did you get it?"

"I used to sell them," Fairman said. "I didn't plan to spend the rest of my life with the Maquis, you know."

"But Chakotay said you were a mercenary."

Fairman snorted. "A lot *he* knows about me. I have plans, Neelix, *big* plans. This replicator is just the start. Once it's up and running—the sky's the limit!"

"I don't know," Neelix said. "Replicated foods are so . . . well, synthetic. They're not good for the digestive system."

"Half the civilized galaxy uses them. Look, I'm happy to cut you in, if that's what you mean."

"I don't think I follow you."

"Oh, come on!" Fairman forced a grin and hoped it didn't look too phony. Neelix was trying to play him for a fool, he thought. "Ten percent—that's fair, isn't it?"

"Ten percent of what? Your replicated foods?"

"No. The *influence.* The *power.* People will pay through the nose for replicated foods . . . chocolate, coffee, tea, everything they've been craving but must do without."

"I understand now," Neelix said. He began to back toward the door. "You're trying to start a black market!"

"Now, that's not a nice way to put it. Think of it as a—well, a *service*. You know how everyone grumbles about your food?"

"What?" Neelix stopped dead in his tracks.

"Grumbles? About my food? It's inconceivable! It's impossible! It's—"

"It's true," Fairman said, nodding. *Now I have him*, he thought. Always appeal to the ego; it was an old salesman's trick. "I'm surprised you haven't noticed. It's because everyone is getting homesick for what they're used to. With my replicator running off an outside power source, we can offer them that alternative . . . and it won't be a drain on the ship. It will make everyone appreciate what you're serving for free in the galley all the more."

"But the captain—"

"Never has to know," Fairman said soothingly. "Nor do Chakotay or Tuvok. B'Elanna, though—I know she's been craving Klingon *gruck* with *zpa*. Think of what it would do for morale to have even *one* replicator up and running full-time."

"I need to think about this," Neelix said. He turned and stepped through the door before Fairman could stop him.

"You'll be back," Paul whispered. "I know you will."

He only hoped it was true.

Tuvok crossed the bridge, nodding to Friend Chakotay, who had returned to duty with his left arm hung in a sling. It must have been a severe fracture, Tuvok reflected, for molecular bonding not to have healed it completely.

The whole bridge crew had changed while he was in the captain's ready room; Friend-Ensigns Kim and Dvorak had been relieved by Friend-Ensigns Iglesias and Basatt; Friends Pietr Ogdanovich and Dmitri Onasis now stood at the weapons and systems stations. Half a dozen men and women from Engineering were working on the consoles.

Tuvok paused to study the work of the engineers. Lieutenant Carey was about to fit a replacement module into the sensor array. His work, usually above reproach, seemed a trifle rushed.

"Mr. Carey," he said.

"Yes, Mr. Tuvok?" Carey asked, head still buried in the console.

"Take greater care with the instruments."

"What—I'm sorry, sir, what do you mean?" He pulled his head out and squinted up, looking bewildered.

"You are being sloppy," Tuvok said.

Carey shook his head slowly, seemingly confused. "Sir?"

"You are being sloppy," he repeated.

"I'm sorry, sir, but I don't understand. In what way?"

"In general," Tuvok said. Couldn't Carey see it? "Sloppiness——" he gestured at the whole console. "Everywhere."

"Aye, sir," Carey said, eyeing him strangely. "I'll take more care."

Chakotay approached. "Is there a problem?" he asked.

"No, Friend-Commander," Tuvok said. "I was

143

merely cautioning Lieutenant Carey to take better care of his instruments. His work is sloppy."

"Carry on," Chakotay said to Carey, "and take more care."

"Aye, sir." Shaking his head, Carey returned to replacing the module.

Tuvok stood with Chakotay and watched the engineer's work for a second. It seemed somewhat improved, he thought. Nodding, he turned and strode to the turbolift, which opened at once. He stepped inside, said, "Deck seven," and waited patiently while it whisked him down. He felt a little hungry and thought a quick bite to eat might make him feel better. He would have to see what Friend Neelix had prepared for dinner. Perhaps another dish with magaberries . . .

When he strolled into the galley, he found Neelix alone with his pots and pans. The small alien brightened at once and came hurrying over.

"Mr. Tuvok! Just the fellow I wanted to see!"

He wrapped his arms around Tuvok and gave him a quick hug. Was this a bonding moment? Tuvok considered it briefly, then decided it wasn't. Neelix had always behaved in this illogical manner.

"What can I do for you, Mr. Neelix?" he asked, gently prying himself free.

"I am posed with a dilemma," Neelix said. He put one arm around Tuvok's shoulder and began to steer him toward the tables in the back of the mess hall. "I require your advice."

"If I can help, I will," Tuvok said. What was this leading up to? Neelix had never come to him for advice before.

"It's like this," Neelix sat at one of the tables, and Tuvok sat opposite him. "One of the crew, Paul Fairman, asked me to provide him with a power supply. It seems he has a small, portable replicator—one he brought over from the Maquis ship—only he needs a power supply to make it run. I found him a power supply, but I'm not sure I should give it to him. In fact, I think it would be a very bad idea."

"I think it would be a good idea," Tuvok said.

"Really?" Neelix said. "Why?"

"Because it's a good idea."

"But he plans to use it for his own gain!"

"No he doesn't," Tuvok said. That seemed the appropriate response.

"He doesn't? But he said—"

"He doesn't," Tuvok said firmly. He was certain that was the correct answer. "I know."

Neelix shook his head, looking confused. "You're certain?" he asked.

"Quite. It is the only logical conclusion."

"Fairman asked me to keep this quiet—" Neelix began.

Tuvok nodded; he often kept Faction secrets. "I understand the need for discretion," he said. "This will be a Faction secret. All right?"

"Is that a Vulcan thing?"

"A Vulcan thing?" Tuvok asked.

"Faction secrets."

"No."

"Ah, Starfleet. Say no more!" Neelix stood, grinning. "Thank you, Mr. Tuvok. You've been an enormous help. I know what to do now!"

"Of course," Tuvok said, also rising. He'd come here to get a quick meal, he reminded himself. "Do you have any more of that excellent goulash?" he asked. "The one with the maga-berries?"

"I just might," Neelix said. "Come on, we'll take a look in the leftover bin."

CHAPTER
16

WHEN SOZOAS REGAINED AWARENESS, HE EXTENDED FIRST one, then another, then another of his head stems. The room echoed oddly and confusion swept over him. He did not know where he was. He extended three more stems and brought the room into sharper focus. Additional wave-signals bouncing back from every surface provided more details: the smoothness of the walls, the sharp angles of the medical tables, the softer floor; the open spaces where air currents breathed.

I am safe, he thought suddenly, relaxing. He recognized this place at last. *I am in sickbay aboard the* Starship Voyager.

But how did he know these things? He hadn't been aboard this ship before, had he?

Tuvok. Friend Tuvok told me.

Then he remembered his Faction-Friends, dead in the warp accelerator's blast. He remembered his little worship tossing wildly in the shock waves, with first one system then another sputtering and dying on him. He remembered calling frantically for help . . . help that he knew would never arrive before he ran out of oxygen. He remembered, in the moments of his greatest despair, when death seemed inevitable, invoking the final great ritual of *sha-tseh*, the great cleansing. He had prepared his body and soul for the afterworld, then lay down to die.

Something now softened those painful memories, however. It felt as though they had happened to someone else, or as though he had perceived the events through someone else's stems. It seemed almost a dream. Yet it had actually happened; of that he was certain.

How much time had passed? He sat up slowly, stems twisting this way and that atop his head, continuing to map everything around him. No clocks vibrated the air currents to tell him the hour. No texture-signs identified the place or its contents.

Movement imposed itself on his attention: the shape he identified as Friend Kes was moving quickly toward him. Briefly he felt a pang of loss as he remembered perceiving her through the sense the Tuvok-self had labeled "sight." He had experienced such "sight" for only a few minutes, but what a glorious few minutes they had been. Colors . . . depth . . . shadow . . . concepts once completely alien now seemed only a fraction's width away.

"How are you?" Friend Kes asked.

The words sounded strange, oddly flat and atonal, with less than half of the richly timbred range of vibrations he would have used in a normal conversation. But strange though those words were, he understood them. He marveled briefly at that. He had never met any aliens before, so how could he understand this one?

Friend Tuvok again. He recalled joining with Friend Tuvok. The strangeness of colors, the richness they added to the sense of texture he already had; it had briefly opened whole new vistas for him. Friend Kes had worn blue and black, and her hair had been pale yellow, he recalled. Friend Doctor had worn blue and black, and had little hair. Now his imagination filled in those colors, mapping them over the intricate patterns and textures that previously had given such an endless variety to his world.

Logically, he thought, joining with Friend Tuvok must have had side effects: he had learned from the Vulcan as the Vulcan had learned from him. It had been a true sharing of souls.

Or perhaps this really *was* the afterlife? He quickly dismissed that theory: Friend Tuvok had been part of his own universe. He had learned that much from their joining. A starship named *Voyager* from a distant sector of space called Alpha Quadrant had rescued him before he had completed *sha-tseh.*

"Can you understand me?" Friend Kes said. "Are you all right, Sozoas?"

He had to communicate. The two tongues in his mouth twisted this way and that as he sought to imitate the sounds these aliens used in their speech. "I—am—fine." The words came out sounding fluted and strange, but Friend Kes seemed to understand them. She gave a sigh and smiled: the strange texture of her teeth, the faint crinkles of her skin as it pulled up around her lips and eyes, these were good things, he thought.

"You speak our language!" she said, sounding surprised and delighted.

"I—must—see—Friend—Tuvok . . . please?" He would soon master their odd method of speech, he thought, curling one tongue around the other. It required a little bit of practice. Their language seemed childishly simple, with less than a hundred distinct noises. He would try leaving his upper tongue still while he spoke with just the lower, and perhaps that would ease the task.

"He will be here soon," she promised. "For now, let me get the doctor." Turning, she hurried toward the small sectioned-off area in the center of the room. Sozoas watched how she walked, the wide sweeping strides, the way her arms thrust out for balance. How did she manage to stay on her feet when she took such huge steps?

A second later Friend Kes returned, trailed by the strangely smooth being, Friend Doctor. Friend Doctor carried a small, equally smooth box, which he held out toward Sozoas. A friendship gift? The box vibrated faintly in Friend Doctor's grip. When Sozoas reached to accept it, Friend Kes took his hands and lowered them. Sozoas turned toward her. Was she bonding? Logically, she shouldn't be offering herself to him: she hadn't taken on the ritual bonding stance of a first or second female (though he knew from his shared memories with Tuvok that she was a female of one sort or another). He extended all six stems toward her in confusion. She didn't seem to understand and offered no explanation. *She's an alien*, he thought. *Perhaps I am missing a subtlety.*

"Your—hands—" he began. "Are—you—?"

"Wait just a second more," she told him. "The doctor is checking to make sure you're all right."

"Thank you—Friend Kes," he said. He had made a mistake. She had not touched him with intent, which certainly made more sense. He wondered how these humanoids would mate, and the Vulcan *pon farr* ritual came to him. *Ritual acceptance of a mate, or combat to win her temporary allegiance. Interesting.* Of course, such a practice made perfect sense for humanoids now that he thought about it. With their rigid logic, they would need times of emotional release, and the mating period seemed appropriate. Friend Kes hadn't been aware that a female touching a male's hands meant she wished to begin the two years of courtship that would win him for her.

"You appear to be well enough," Friend Doctor finally said, lowering his box. "Can you stand?"

"Yes." Sozoas climbed down from the medical table and stood before them. His stems came level with Friend Kes's chin and Friend Doctor's chest. Slowly he turned, raising his arms, showing them the fitness of his body. He flexed himself joint by joint, then bowed low. "Your care—has been most—excellent, Friend Doctor."

"We do have a certain standard to maintain," Friend Doctor said. "Is there anything we can get you to eat or drink?"

"Perhaps—" He hesitated. "Water?"

* * * *

Tuvok was just finishing his leftover Verosan goulash when his badge chirped. The meal had been a delight; he savored the colors of the fruits and vegetables as much as the flavor. He'd never really noticed how important colors were to food before, but now he found they added a depth to the enjoyment that he had previously never experienced.

He tapped his badge absently. "Tuvok here," he said.

"Janeway here," he heard Leader Janeway say. "The doctor just informed me that the Sperian has regained consciousness. Please join me in the sickbay."

"On my way," Tuvok said, rising.

Tom Paris stood outside Marta Dvorak's cabin, hesitating. He'd never gotten anywhere with her before, but today had been particularly exhausting. A battle that had almost gotten them killed, hull breaches, double shifts . . . he still felt the tension in his neck and back. He needed to unwind . . . and he suspected she needed to unwind, too. Why couldn't they do it together? Something about Marta's face, something about her eyes, something about her voice, drew him to her like a moth to a flame.

He made up his mind. It was now or never. He stepped forward and heard the computer chime his presence.

"Who is it?" a soft voice asked.

"Tom Paris," he said.

The door slid open. Marta had changed into a filmy white nightgown and let down her long silky hair. Her skin almost glowed in the soft light spilling from her cabin, and her blue eyes seemed to sparkle. He'd never seen her looking so beautiful. He didn't think he'd ever seen *anyone* looking so beautiful.

She leaned up against the doorframe and Tom caught a hint of an alien perfume, delicate, softly spiced with the scents of exotic flowers. He leaned forward and inhaled slowly.

"What can I do for you, Lieutenant?" Marta asked, suddenly very businesslike.

"I was hoping you might join me for a picnic," he said. He grinned and held up a datachip. "I've checked and the holosuite's free. It's also one of the few systems running at full power."

"It sounds intriguing," she said, "but I'm afraid I can't." She moved a little to the side and glanced over her shoulder. "I'm afraid I've already got plans for the evening."

Tom followed her gaze . . . to where Harry Kim sat with a wine glass in his hand. Harry raised his glass in salute.

Tom felt himself blush. "I—uh——" he began.

"Thanks anyway." Marta stepped back and the door slid shut.

Tom slapped the bulkhead wall. Harry had beaten him to the punch, it seemed. The kid was learning. Then he grinned a bit lopsidedly. What could he expect? He *was* learning from a master.

Whistling, he turned and strolled up the corridor.

Kathryn Janeway waited outside the sickbay for Tuvok. She felt a little apprehensive, but tried to hide it: she didn't have time for that sort of thing. What was keeping her security officer?

Finally Tuvok came striding around the gently

curving corridor. He looked much his old self, she thought; his color was good, his head back, his gaze strong and level.

He strode up and stopped neatly in front of her.

"Are you ready, Leader?"

Her brow creased. Leader? It seemed a bit odd, but she didn't have time for that now.

"Yes," she said. "And you?"

"Affirmative."

She took a deep breath and stepped forward. The door opened and she found herself in sickbay. The Sperian—Sozoas, she reminded herself; that was his name—stood to the left, talking with Kes and the doctor. Sozoas looked much improved; although his skin was still a mottled gray, the tendrils on top of his head now writhed constantly, and his every movement seemed strong and surer.

"V'peth sem t'tar," the alien said, turning toward her, his voice a trill of sound. "Friend Tuvok. Leader Janeway. *S'path tzi nar loth.*"

How did he know her? The mind-meld must have given him as much information as it had given Tuvok, she thought. She glanced over at the Vulcan, who bowed low from the waist. She hesitated a second and then did the same. She had to rely on Tuvok's instincts now, she thought.

"I am pleased to encounter you once again, Friend Tuvok," Sozoas said in a lightly accented English. "Our joining has expanded my worldview."

"As it has mine," Tuvok said. "I note that you have mastered our language."

"Se'peth na ho-tkso," Sozoas said.

"Zha na ho-tkso," Tuvok replied. "As I have mastered yours. It was a good sharing, Friend Sozoas." He turned. "I wish to present Leader Janeway, who commands this ship."

"Leader Janeway." Sozoas bowed to her a second time.

"Sozoas," she said, "I am pleased to meet you." Tuvok nodded imperceptibly, so she bowed once more in response. Things were going better than she'd dare hope.

"You have attained the rank of Friend?" Sozoas went on. "That is how our shared memories place you . . . and yet you are Leader?"

Janeway glanced at Tuvok, who seemed to purposefully be avoiding her gaze. She considered Tuvok a friend, but they'd never quite managed to put their relationship into words. Still, it was nice to know how he truly felt about her, after all these years, it warmed her inside.

"That is correct," she said slowly to Sozoas. "I am privileged to call Tuvok a friend. I would like to be your friend as well."

"In our society Friendships may overlap different ranks," Tuvok explained to Sozoas. "It is a ritual custom."

"Exactly so," Janeway said quickly, following his lead. "I would be happy to rank you as a Friend."

"When in Rome—that is the human saying?" Sozoas asked.

Janeway laughed. "Yes. Yes, that's correct." She glanced around sickbay. Kes and the doctor, though they'd quietly moved out of the way, appeared to be listening raptly. No, she thought, sickbay did not seem the appropriate setting for this, the first meeting between their species.

"Doctor," she said, "is Sozoas free to leave?"

"Of course," the doctor said. "He seems to be in fine shape physically, considering he has been unconscious for most of a day, injected with psychotropes, and undergone a Vulcan mind-meld. A trifle dehydrated, but a glass of water fixed that."

"Very well," Janeway said, making up her mind.

"Sozoas, if you'll follow me, we'll adjourn to a conference room."

"Agreed, Leader Janeway. I believe we have much to discuss. Logically, many benefits await both of our peoples."

"This way." She turned toward the door and he shuffled after her. His short legs prevented him from walking quickly, so she adjusted her pace to match.

She couldn't believe Neelix had called the Sperians argumentative. Sozoas seemed to be bending over backward to be accommodating. This seemed one of the most promising first contacts they'd had in the Delta Quadrant.

Tuvok had lingered a moment in sickbay. She paused in the doorway to wait for him.

"Kes," he said, "I find the colors you are wearing visually appealing. Thank you for the experience."

"Thank you for the compliment," Kes replied happily, beaming at him. "You know, Tuvok, that's the first nice thing you've said to me." She laughed lightly. "If you're not careful, you'll make Neelix jealous. . . ."

"Jealousy would be illogical in this instance," Tuvok said. "I am already quite happily mated." He turned and started toward the door, but Janeway raised one hand to stop him. He regarded her quizzically for a moment.

"Stay here for a full medical checkup, Tuvok," she said. She turned to the holographic doctor. "Do you concur?"

"Yes," he said. "This is the second instance of abnormal behavior I've noticed in Mr. Tuvok since the mind-meld, Captain."

Tuvok frowned. "This delay is neither necessary nor desirable, Captain."

"I think it is," she said.

"You are wrong," he insisted.

"That's a direct order, Mr. Tuvok."

"But you are wrong," he said again.

"The decision is no longer yours," she said. It wasn't like him to argue this way. She knew now, without a bit of doubt, that something had affected him. She just hoped it wasn't the mind-meld. If any permanent damage had been done, she'd never forgive herself.

"But you are wrong," Tuvok said for the third time.

"If so," she said, "the doctor will give you a clean bill of health."

"That's right," the doctor said, taking Tuvok's arm. "Let's start you on the medical scanner."

"I believe a blood biopsy would be more appropriate," Tuvok said.

"But—" the doctor began.

Tuvok set his feet. "A blood biopsy," he insisted.

"I know more about this equipment and how to run it than you do," the doctor said. "And I believe I outrank you in sickbay, Mr. Tuvok."

"But we are not in sickbay, not properly."

"Yes we are," the doctor began, a trifle hotly.

Janeway sighed. Another problem—and unfortunately one that remained beyond her power to solve. She'd have to rely on the doctor.

"This way," she said to Sozoas. "I'm sorry you had to witness this display. Tuvok seems to be suffering some ill effects of the mind-meld."

"What manner of ill effects?" Sozoas asked.

Janeway gave him a quick glance out of the corner of her eye and found that all the tendrils on his head had extended themselves toward her. She seemed to have his undivided attention. Hadn't he noticed Tuvok's challenging, argumentative, almost childlike, and completely un-Vulcan temper tantrum? Perhaps he had, only it hadn't registered as anything unusual, she thought.

"It's nothing important," she assured him. "I'm sure he'll be back to duty in no time."

"Let us hope so," Sozoas said. "Logically, he is an essential part of your crew and cannot be long detained from duty."

As Sozoas said that, the answer suddenly clicked into place for her. If all Sperians were argumentative by nature, perhaps a little of his personality had become imprinted on Tuvok's mind . . . and perhaps a little of Tuvok's orderly, agreeable nature had been imprinted on Sozoas. It was a trade that might prove beneficial in the short term, but would definitely be a liability to her if it turned out to be permanent.

She'd take advantage of it now and let the doctor try to straighten out Tuvok in the meantime.

"I have known Tuvok for many years," she said, stepping into the corridor and turning to the right. Sozoas followed a little more slowly. "Based on our Friendship, he was not acting in his usual precise manner."

"Ah," said Sozoas. "I understand."

"Here we are." She stopped in front of a pair of doors, which slid open smoothly. Inside, a round table with comfortable high-backed chairs took up the center of the room. A single large viewport looked out into space. The warp-accelerator tube turned slowly between the red giant and the white dwarf. Any other time she might have found it a beautiful sight, but now she only had thoughts of business.

She sat, motioning for Sozoas to do likewise. He went at once to Tuvok's usual place to the right of her chair and sat. His stance, his every gesture, now reminded her of Tuvok. It was eerie.

Taking a deep breath, she launched into the story of how they had picked up Sozoas's distress call, then all they had encountered in the system. She ended with B'Elanna's discovery of sabotage aboard the warp-accelerator tube, then the running battle that had left the three Sperian ships disabled.

"Has full life support been restored to all the three ships?" he asked.

"I'll check." She tapped her badge. "Janeway to bridge."

"Chakotay here, Captain," he answered.

"What is the status of the three Sperian ships?"

"All three have at least minimal life support restored. We are monitoring their repairs. Navigational controls seem to be their highest priority, since gravimetric tides are starting to work on them."

Sozoas stood and moved to the viewport, gazing out into the void. "Is it possible for me to communicate directly with my people?"

"Of course," Janeway said. "We can set up a comm link from here, if they'll receive the signal."

"They will," he said firmly.

Janeway swung a communications station around to face him. "Janeway to communications officer," she said.

"Ensign Iglesias," a man's voice answered.

"Prepare to hail the three Sperian ships in five minutes. Route the signal through this console."

"Aye, Captain," he said. "Ready."

Janeway turned to Sozoas. "Let me check on Tuvok first," she said. "I would like him here as well, if possible."

She didn't add, *To keep track of everything you say.* Whether he was fit for duty or not, he was the only one who could understand the Sperian language.

Sozoas seemed to pick up on her intentions. "Of course, Friend Janeway," he said. "You must safeguard your position. That is standard procedure. We will wait for Friend Tuvok."

CHAPTER

17

KES WATCHED WITH MINGLED SURPRISE AND AMUSEMENT
as Tuvok and the doctor argued through every step
of the examination. She'd known the doctor had
an obstinate streak running through his programming; it was part of what made him an effective phy-
sician. He didn't give up no matter what argument
Tuvok presented. He simply changed tactics and kept
going.

That strategy seemed remarkably effective. Tuvok
underwent the series of tests the doctor proposed, just
not in the order the doctor would have run them on
his own.

Strangely, the blood biopsy turned up nothing
unusual when she ran it. Neither did the cerebral
scan, or the bioscan, or any of the other tests they
administered. Kes took a mental step back and tried

to regard Tuvok in a fresh light—a thought exercise that Neelix used on occasion. According to every indication, Tuvok was in splendid physical shape for a Vulcan of his age.

"As I told you," Tuvok said, pulling his shirt back on. "This examination was unnecessary."

"Then how do you explain your unusually emotional responses?" the doctor countered. "When was the last time you complimented another crewman's clothing?"

"About five-point-two minutes ago."

"And the time before that?"

Tuvok seemed to plunge deep into thought. He did not answer. Kes, too, tried to recall the last time she'd heard him compliment someone . . . and found she couldn't. She'd assumed it wasn't in his nature until now.

"I cannot recall another instance," Tuvok finally admitted.

"Exactly my point!" the doctor went on. "It's atypical behavior, which indicates something wrong. We have eliminated physical problems. That leaves a mental one."

"Unless," Tuvok said, "I merely had not noticed Kes's clothing until today, at which point the response becomes entirely appropriate."

"I'm not sure it's all that important," Kes said to break up the new argument she felt certain was starting. "But why shouldn't Tuvok compliment the color of my clothing if he likes it?"

"It is not," the doctor said slowly, "a matter of like or dislike. Vulcans simply do not compliment people as he complimented you. It's an emotional and highly subjective response."

"It is," Tuvok said calmly, "a statement of fact."

"Do you remember your father?" Kes asked him suddenly. Perhaps she could steer Tuvok toward the true answer and let him work things out for himself. That's what Neelix would have done.

"Of course," Tuvok said.

"Was he as logical and in control of his emotions as you are?"

"More so. I have always strived to live up to the example he set."

"Then you know him well enough to predict what he would say under situations similar to those you encountered today . . . like seeing me in these clothes . . . like having Captain Janeway and the doctor keep you here for examination."

Tuvok frowned. "I believe I see your point," he said slowly. "My responses do appear unusual when compared to the Vulcan standard as represented by my father." He paused as if searching deep within himself for answers. "These events bear further consideration," he admitted.

"I would suggest," the doctor said, "that you monitor your own words and actions carefully over the next twenty-four hours. Compare them in your mind to what you would expect another Vulcan such as your father or another authority figure to say or do in similar circumstances. If you begin to fall into any pattern that appears to deviate from the Vulcan norm, stop and consider carefully why you are doing it."

"I will attempt that," Tuvok said.

"Then I see no reason to keep you from duty," the doctor said. "However, I would like you to report here again in twenty-four hours for a follow-up examination."

The ship's intercom chirped and Captain Janeway's voice said, "Doctor, is Tuvok able to report for duty? I need him here now."

"He's not well, but I believe he is fit enough for limited duty—if little mental stress is involved."

"Thank you, Doctor. Have him report to me in conference room four. Janeway out."

"You heard the captain," the doctor said. "Back to work, Mr. Tuvok—but don't forget what I said."

Janeway's mouth went dry as Tuvok entered the conference room and slid efficiently into the seat opposite Sozoas. He looked . . . distant, somehow. Not himself, but not the argumentative person he had been changing into, either. Had the doctor done something to him? Or was his mental illness progressing to another stage? She'd have to monitor him carefully, she thought.

"I assume," Tuvok said as if nothing had happened, "that you have already made preparations to contact the three Sperian ships." He folded his hands on top of the conference table and looked inquiringly at her.

"Yes," Janeway said. "But how are you feeling, Mr. Tuvok? Are you certain you're up to this?"

"Yes, Captain. I wish to . . . apologize for the incident in sickbay. It will not happen again."

He's clamped down on himself, she realized. To all outward appearances his self-control was complete. *He's put an iron grip on his thoughts and emotions. He won't let anything go wrong at this meeting no matter how much it tears him up inside. It means that much to him.*

It was exactly what she would have done in his place, she knew. And the best thing she could do for him would be to get on with their work. That way he could bury himself in it, and perhaps slowly the old Tuvok, the Tuvok she knew and trusted, would emerge once more.

She touched her badge. "Hail the three ships," she said.

"Done, Captain," Iglesias said.

"Proceed," she said to Sozoas. She'd have to trust to Sozoas and Tuvok now to sort things out.

The Sperian leaned forward. *"Na braszh,"* he said. Strange whistles and chirps accompanied the words. *"Azhact na braszh Sozoas."*

This had better work, Janeway thought suddenly. If she'd sacrificed Tuvok's mind for nothing, she didn't know what she'd do. She swallowed.

"He said 'Attention, Faction-Friends,'" Tuvok announced, "this is subLeader Sozoas.'"

"Pra-toth na sz'asa," Sozoas went on, and Tuvok provided a running translation for both sides.

"I am in charge of engineering on the warp-acceleration project," Sozoas said. "Reply if you can hear this transmission."

"We receive your message with joy," came the reply from the lead Sperian ship. "We believed you were all dead. Have you been captured by the enemy, subLeader? Are there other survivors of the massacre?"

"No, there are no other survivors," Sozoas said. "I

have been rescued by new Faction-Friends from the United Federation of Planets, a distant alliance. I am now aboard their starship *Voyager*. That is of little importance, however. I have vital information which must be relayed to our Faction Leader. The warp-acceleration project has been destroyed by sabotage from an unknown Faction or subFaction. The warp-accelerator tube was turned upon our space city as a weapon."

"How is this possible?"

"I do not yet know. You must return to base and make my report to our Leaders. I will remain here to investigate further."

"Our ships will remain also," the other ship's captain said.

"No," Sozoas said.

"Yes."

"No."

"Yes."

"No. I invoke my privilege as subLeader to end this discussion."

The other Sperian bowed from the waist. "As you command, subLeader."

The yes-ing and no-ing seemed almost a ritual in this instance, Janeway thought. It seemed the Sperians had found ways to get around the argumentative nature of their society. If only Neelix knew, he might have felt differently about dealing with them— he could be very . . .

"How long until your ships are repaired?" Sozoas went on.

"The *A-Zha-Gor* will have warp capabilities in eight hours. The *A-Zir-Toin* will have warp capabilities in seven hours. The *A-Zna-Tus* will have warp capabilities in nine hours."

"That is acceptable. Continue work. Advise me when all three ships are warp-capable. SubLeader Sozoas out."

"Thank you," Janeway said. "I believe we have made major steps forward here."

Sozoas inclined his head. "It was the only logical thing to do," he said. "We must seek the true enemy. Friend Janeway, is it possible to have the black-box mechanism from the accelerator tube brought aboard your ship?"

"It should be," she said.

"I wish to examine it," he said. "Perhaps it will provide us with information about who designed and implemented it."

Janeway glanced at Tuvok. "Your recommendations, Mr. Tuvok?"

"I think," he said slowly, as if weighing his words carefully, "that caution is indicated here, Captain. We did not disturb the black box earlier because we did not want to raise alarms. At present, *Voyager* is not ready for action of any kind."

"I agree," she said. She turned to Sozoas. "You're going to have to wait until our repairs are completed. We should be finished before your three ships are operational."

"That is acceptable," he said. "Perhaps there is something else we can do in the meantime. I believe your ship monitors and records all communications it picks up?"

"Of course," Janeway said. It was standard procedure: the computer automatically recorded and stored a full day's worth of signals as part of the operational log. They were almost never used except to analyze events leading up to disasters that left starships dead or destroyed.

"You want to listen to them," Tuvok said.

"Why?" Janeway said. Then she understood.

"Coded transmissions designed to blend in with background noise!" she said.

"Precisely," Sozoas said. "I know several different Faction and subFaction codes. We may be able to identify the saboteurs after all."

CHAPTER

18

NEELIX SHIFTED THE POWER SUPPLY TO HIS LEFT ARM AS he strolled down the corridor. He hoped he wasn't making a mistake. What Fairman had said about the crew complaining about his food had really hurt him, but now that Fairman had mentioned it, he could kind of see what the fellow meant. The *phu* and the *paga*-root were both acquired tastes if you hadn't been raised on them, and he'd certainly caught several people giving their plates strange looks over the last few weeks.

Besides, if a home-style meal or two would boost morale, it was his duty to look into it. Perhaps it wouldn't be so bad. If Fairman doled out the replicated food in an orderly and efficient manner—and much of the Federation seemed to run in an orderly and efficient manner, as far as he could tell—then it would be like giving the crew extra replicator rations. Which was definitely a good thing.

He reached Fairman's cabin, rapped twice, and said, "I'm here."

"Come in, come in!" Fairman was on his feet looking expectantly at the door when it slid open. "Neelix, is that . . . ?"

"Your power supply." Neelix held it up like a prize.

"Wonderful! I can't tell you how much this means to me!" Fairman took the box and held it out at arm's length, turning it this way and that. Slowly he frowned. "This looks like a standard Federation coupling, but I've never seen anything like this unit before. Where did you get it?"

"It's salvage from the Sperian space city. I adapted it for use with Federation equipment."

"And the output levels . . . ?"

"Fall well within Federation standards."

"Then I'll give it a try." Fairman crossed to the closet and pulled out a bright red box about half the size of a standard replicator. The front opening, about twice as wide as it was tall, would hold a single plate of food and not much else, Neelix thought with a measure of disappointment. Somehow he'd expected something more, something bigger and more impressive.

Fairman carried the little replicator to a small table. He spun it around and plugged the Sperian power supply into the back.

Nothing happened. *Did I do my adjustments wrong?* Neelix wondered. He searched his memory. No, everything had seemed to check out all right. And the power supply had checked out according to the ship's computer-run diagnostics. If anything, the problem had to lie with Fairman's replicator.

"Is it broken?" he asked.

"It's just the standard power-up sequence for a portable," Fairman said. "Here we go."

The front panel of the replicator abruptly lit up with a steady green light. Fairman touched a button, said, "Hot chocolate," and a second later a mug of a steaming brown liquid materialized inside.

Fairman pulled it out, raised it, sniffed appreciatively, then offered it to Neelix. "Here you go. First one's yours. Be careful, it's hot."

Neelix accepted it a little suspiciously. He'd once heard Harry Kim mention hot chocolate as a delicacy he missed, but he'd never imagined it was a beverage. He sniffed once. It had a sweet aroma, quite different from the coffee Captain Janeway and a few of the crewmen enjoyed with their replicator rations.

He glanced over at Fairman, who was watching him expectantly. Well, he thought, he might as well get it over with. He sipped.

It was too hot, that was his first impression. His second was that it had an almost cloying sweetness, but a pinch of bitter *hacamb*-tree bark or perhaps finely grated *emf* leaves would fix it right up. Yes, this hot chocolate definitely had possibilities.

"What's it made from?" he asked. If humans considered it such a delicacy, perhaps he could make it himself from materials available in this quadrant. Of course, he'd have to fix the problem with the flavor, but that was minor.

"A replicator," Fairman said.

"No, I mean originally. What did humans make it from before there were replicators?"

Fairman blinked. "I have no idea."

"Never mind, I'll ask the computer later." He shook his head sadly; humans could be so clueless when it came to food. Sometimes he thought they didn't care what they shoved in their mouths. Why, he could serve them yellow *porchuk* and they'd gobble it up like boiled *phu.*

"Now," Fairman said, rubbing his hands together, "we're in business, partner!"

"If you'll excuse me," Neelix said, "I have to begin preparations for breakfast."

"Anything you say." Fairman didn't look up from his replicator. "Scrambled eggs and sage sausage!" he said. The little machine began to whir, and then a plate appeared inside. Fairman removed it. "Coffee, double sugar, double cream!"

Shaking his head, Neelix left. Somehow, he had a feeling he'd just made a colossal error.

Pablo Iglesias studied the Sperian from the corner of his eye as he called up the ship's communications logs from the time *Voyager* entered the Arbuk system. Harry Kim had briefed him about the situation when he took over the communications station, and he'd seen the transmission Harry had picked up, but it hadn't prepared him for seeing Sozoas in person. The Sperian looked even stranger and more unsettling than he had on the ship's monitors. It was the lack of eyes, Pablo thought, that did it. The sensory stems atop the Sperian's head provided much the same information, according to Tuvok, but to a human like him, they offered no clues as to the thoughts going on inside. He'd never realized before how important eyes were in judging people.

"Ready for playback," he said.

"Begin," Tuvok said.

He activated the switch. Static from the two stars, punctuated by the background hiss of radiation from open space, came from the speakers. It sounded like nothing special to him, but Sozoas began gesturing at once.

"Abn z'rachit!" he said.

Tuvok replied in the same language, and Pablo watched cluelessly as they carried on a strange glottal, whistley conversation in front of him. He wished he had a running translation. Still, Tuvok would fill him in if it became important, he knew.

At last, nodding, Tuvok turned to him and said, "Ensign, switch to current background noise and continue monitoring with Sozoas. If he hears anything unusual, summon me."

"Aye, sir," Pablo said.

Tuvok turned and, without another word of explanation, strode to the captain's ready room. He entered.

Pablo turned back to Sozoas. "Can you tell me what you heard on the tape?" he asked.

"Signals from the Military Faction," the alien said.

Janeway motioned Tuvok forward as she listened to the last of Lieutenant Carey's report.

"Thank you, Mr. Carey," she said. "It's nice to hear good news for a change. Keep it up."

"Aye, Captain," Carey said, and signed off.

"Good news?" Tuvok asked.

"Very." Janeway leaned back in her seat. She felt old and tired suddenly; this had turned into a long night. "The hull breach has been patched, at least temporarily. We'll have warp engines on-line within the hour. We have full shields and full weapons now, plus impulse power, all well ahead of schedule. The transporter will be working in fifteen minutes. And we should have most of the secondary systems back up within the hour."

"Good news indeed, then."

"What did you and Sozoas learn from the ship's tapes?"

Tuvok inclined his head. "The transmissions seem to have originated from the Military Faction, as we suspected."

"Can't you tell for certain?"

"Negative. The Military subFaction of the Tech Faction uses a nearly identical code. The only way to ascertain the guilty party will be for Sozoas to examine the control mechanism inside the tube."

Janeway nodded slowly. "Very well. Now that we have our primary defensive systems back on-line, have B'Elanna remove that box she found. Have it beamed aboard as soon as possible."

"Yes, Captain." He turned to go.

"And Tuvok," she called.

He paused. "Yes, Captain?"

"Get some rest. That's an order."

He opened his mouth, and Janeway knew he wanted to argue that he was fine, but then his inner control clamped down hard. He merely said, "Yes, Captain. As soon as I implement your orders."

Janeway stifled a yawn herself. Time for her to turn in, too, or she'd be dead on her feet.

B'Elanna bit her lip and heaved, using pure muscle to rip the black box free of its housing. She'd spent half an hour carefully rerouting microconnections and power feeds. Then she'd spent another half hour removing spot welds to free the box. When she finished, though, it stubbornly refused to slide free of its housing. So she resorted to good old-fashioned brute force.

With a ripping sound, the box tore free. When she examined the back, she discovered the residue from what looked like a plastic-based adhesive. It had been glued in place.

"Just so it's intact," she murmured.

She raised her tricorder and took a quick scan. Now the box showed no activity: it was neither transmitting nor receiving information. Somehow she'd interrupted it. *And I was so careful,* she thought. So much for her painstaking attention to detail.

She's better report in, she knew. As quickly as she could she donned her helmet and went back outside. There, without the interference, she called home: "B'Elanna to *Voyager.*"

"Voyager here. Go ahead, Lieutenant." It was Pablo Iglesias's voice.

"Tell Captain Janeway I accidentally broke the link between the control box and the saboteurs. The box is ready to beam over."

"Janeway here," came the captain's voice a second later. "Are you ready to beam out?"

"Negative," she said. "I want to slave control of the tube's thrusters over to the *Voyager* first."

"How long will that take?"

"Another ten minutes."

"Make it so. Then get over here. If we have unexpected company, I don't want you stranded over there again. Janeway out."

B'Elanna released the control box down and watched it drift slowly away from her. She signaled *Voyager* again: "B'Elanna to transporter room. Lock on to these coordinates." She fed them the reading from the tricorder. "Beam it over."

The control box disappeared in a shimmer of light.

Now, she thought, to wrap things up. Unraveling the sabotage had given her a good grasp of the underlying principles of the warp-acceleration tube. It would be an easy matter to switch control from the now nonexistent space city to a frequency used by the Federation. Just a few minor circuits to alter, a few controls to hook back up, and it would be done.

She headed back inside.

The door chimed softly. Yawning and rubbing the sleep from his eyes, Harry Kim sat up. "Light," he said, and a soft glow lit his cabin. He'd been asleep, what, twenty minutes? No, according to the chronometer, almost six hours. It just felt like twenty minutes.

Yawning again, he slid out of bed, cinched a robe around his waist, and headed for the door. This had better be good, he thought.

"Open," he said, and the door slid aside.

INCIDENT AT ARBUK

It was Paul Fairman, looking remarkably chipper. He had a cart of some kind covered with a white cloth.

"What do you want?" Harry demanded.

"I'm sorry if I disturbed you," Fairman said with a grin, "but I have something that might interest you. May I come in?"

Harry yawned once more, but stepped back. "Okay, but make it quick. I pulled a double shift yesterday." *Might as well take a look,* he thought, *as long as I'm up. What could he possibly have that would interest me?*

Fairman wheeled his cart in and, when the door closed, whipped off the covering. Harry felt his eyes widen in surprise as he recognized the replicator. It was a Reflux, just like his mother had . . . only hers was quite a bit larger.

"Where did you get that?" Harry asked.

"Never mind the questions," Fairman said with a grin. "I got the final part I needed from someone pretty high up. Suffice to say, it's here, it's real, and it works. Since it has an external power supply, it's not a drain on the ship's resources. So it can be used as much as I want."

It had to be someone pretty high up, Harry thought. The captain wouldn't be involved in any secret like this, and Commander Chakotay clearly disliked Fairman. Who else could have wrangled a private replicator aboard? Paris, maybe?

Harry licked his lips. "I take it you've brought it here for a reason."

"You got it, kid." Fairman grinned again. "Pick your favorite food."

"What's the catch?"

"No catch. Whatever you want, whatever you've been craving, name it and it's yours."

"Hot chocolate," Harry said.

It materialized inside the replicator. Hesitantly, Harry reached in, removed the steaming mug, and took a small sip. Delicious, exactly like his mother used to make. He'd been craving hot chocolate for weeks, and he savored the smell, the taste, the every sensation.

Fairman covered the replicator and wheeled it toward the door. "Let me know if you need anything else," he said. "I have other samples to deliver."

"Uh, wait a second," Harry said. He felt his stomach rumble faintly. "Since you're here and all . . . blueberry pancakes with butter and hot syrup go great with hot chocolate."

"Coming right up." He uncovered the replicator and produced pancakes exactly as Harry had asked. When Harry reached for them, though, Fairman held them out of reach. "There's still the matter of price," he said.

"Price?" Harry frowned. "What do you mean?"

Fairman smiled, and suddenly Harry found it wasn't so much a happy expression as a predatory one. "Kid, only the first one's free."

"How much?" Harry asked suspiciously.

"Just a favor sometime. Nothing big. But I'd like to know I can count on you if I have a problem. In fact, I know just what I want this time: your promise not to mention our little friend here"—he patted the top of the replicator—"to anyone else."

The smell of the pancakes got to him. His mouth

was watering, his stomach rumbled, and suddenly Harry had to have those blueberry pancakes. He couldn't help himself.

"Mister, you've got a deal," he said.

Fairman shook hands solemnly with him. "Enjoy it, Harry," he said. "I think this is the start of a beautiful friendship."

Tuvok slid the black box across the conference table toward Sozoas. "It came from the Military Faction itself, if my analysis is correct," he said.

"Yes," Sozoas said. Janeway watched as he ran his six fingertips over the device, then abruptly pushed it away. "The markings are unmistakable."

"Unless—" Tuvok began. He broke off abruptly, and Janeway realized he'd almost begun another argument: the effects of the mind-meld again. His face took on a rigid expression, as if carved from stone, and he began to stare off into the distance. This had to be eating him up inside, she knew.

"Markings?" Janeway asked to break the awkward silence. The box looked completely featureless to her.

"Sperians see in textures rather than colors," Tuvok said. "Touch the box and you will feel the markings."

Janeway pulled it closer to her and ran her fingertips across its surface. Several areas felt like sandpaper; others were smooth as glass. Almost like the Braille language they used to use on Earth, she thought, only infinitely more subtle.

"How does this identify the Military Faction as the culprit?" she asked. "What does it say?"

Tuvok leaned forward and traced the rough area's outline with one finger. "This symbol marks it as a product of the Miir Shtat Laboratories, which are—which are—" He broke off, a puzzled look on his face.

"I cannot remember what they are."

"Perhaps the effects of the mind-meld are wearing off," Janeway said softly.

"A distinct possibility, Captain."

Sozoas said, "The Miir Shtat Laboratories are under the Military Faction's direct control. Anything produced there would have to have been commissioned and approved by them. This device is all the evidence I require."

"But why would they go to such extremes to make sure your project failed?" Janeway asked. "Murdering so many is barbarous!"

"If the project failed," Sozoas said. "They could rightly assume we would abandon the acceleration tube here. They could move in, take over whatever equipment and installations remained in this system, and continue the research on their own."

"What will happen now?" she asked.

"Assuming I am not ritually assassinated and the control box stolen, I will stand before the Council of Factions and state our complaint. They will have no choice but to sanction the Military Faction."

"Ritually assassinated?"

"Of course. If the Military Faction kills me, there will be no witnesses to their crime left."

"Captain," Tuvok said slowly, "if the Council follows the usual pattern of judgments in cases such as this one, three members of the Military Faction will be executed for every member of the Tech Faction who was murdered."

"Innocent people—" Janeway said, startled. The

guilty should be punished, of course, but to arbitrarily kill just to add up to a certain number of deaths appalled her.

"Those chosen for execution will buy their lives by shifting their primary allegiance to the Tech Faction," Sozoas said. "There have not been any actual executions in many, many centuries. However, there were more than eighty-five thousand Sperians aboard our research center. This will be a significant restructuring of Faction power."

"I must recommend placing the ship on alert status," Tuvok said. "The Military Faction may choose to act against us, rather than let the judgment proceed against them with both a witness and evidence."

She tapped her comm badge. "Captain to bridge. Chakotay, move the ship away from the tube at impulse power. I want more distance between us and it in case other ships show up. Go to yellow alert."

"Aye, Captain," she heard Chakotay say.

But instead of the amber light she'd expected, red alert sounded. Chakotay's voice came through to her. "Captain to the bridge. A new Sperian vessel is approaching—it looks like a warship."

CHAPTER
19

"ON MY WAY," SHE SAID. SHE TURNED TO SOZOAS. "Please come with me."

"But," he whistled, "I am quite comfortable here."

"It's urgent—" she began. Then she broke off. If the side effects of the mind-meld had also begun to wear off on Tuvok, perhaps they had also begun to wear off on Sozoas. That would make him argumentative and quarrelsome, and she didn't have time for that right now.

To Tuvok, she said, "Get him to the bridge as quickly as you can. Use force if you have to."

"Yes, Captain."

Turning, she strode out to the turbolift. A warship she'd made sure most of *Voyager*'s repairs were finished before allowing B'Elanna to remove the warp accelerator's remote-control device. With their eyes—so to speak—gone, of course the Military Faction had no option left but to make an appearance.

The turbolift stopped. When she stepped onto the bridge, Janeway glanced at the forward viewscreen and found an image of the new Sperian vessel. It was approaching quickly.

"Status, Chakotay?" she asked.

"The new ship is heading for the three disabled Sperian vessels," he said. "Its weapons are armed."

"Perhaps they have also come in response to Sozoas's distress call," she said, though she didn't believe it for an instant. "For the moment we must give them the benefit of the doubt."

"They're locking photon torpedoes on the closest Sperian target," Ensign Dvorak said from the weapons console. "They are preparing to fire."

So much for that theory, Janeway thought. She said, "Full impulse power, Mr. Paris. Put us between that warship and the disabled vessels. They're going to have to go through us first."

"Aye, Captain," Tom said, his hands moving deftly across the controls.

Voyager leaped forward. In seconds they had maneuvered between the oncoming vessel and the three helpless Tech Faction ships. The newcomer was huge—two or three times larger than *Voyager*—and it consisted of a large silver sphere with two smaller spheres stuck on either side. The smaller spheres had openings in them that reminded her distinctly of gun ports.

"They are decelerating," Marta said. "Weapons systems have locked on to us instead."

"Raise shields," Janeway said. Were there any more ships out there that she didn't know about? It was a distinct possibility. "Where did they come from?" she asked.

"They just emerged from warp," Chakotay said. "We weren't able to pick them up until they were almost on top of us."

"Have we received any transmissions from them yet, Mr. Kim?" she asked.

"Not yet, Captain," Harry said.

Janeway frowned. Their motives seemed transparently obvious . . . perhaps too much so. Or was she giving them more credit than they were due?

"Open hailing frequencies," she said.

"Hailing frequencies open," Harry said.

She stood and moved forward to face the viewscreen. "This is Captain Kathryn Janeway of the Federation *Starship Voyager* to the approaching Sperian vessel. Please identify yourself."

There was no reply. Somehow, Janeway wasn't surprised; she hadn't expected one, given the problems they'd had so far communicating with the Sperians . . . and given the shoot-first attitude displayed by the three Tech Faction ships.

She turned to Chakotay once more. "What are their capabilities?" she asked.

"We can outmaneuver them, but they outgun us, Captain. I don't think we could win a heads-up firefight."

"Then we'll have to avoid one at all costs. Mr. Paris, prepare to execute evasive maneuver Omega Twelve on my order." That would take them under and around the attacking ship, firing all the time. If they really could run rings around the Sperian vessel, she intended to use that advantage to its fullest. She had no intention of sitting still while they shot her ship to pieces. The Sperians on the three disabled vessels were depending on her, as well as her own crew.

"Aye, Captain," Tom said, beginning to lock in the maneuver.

"They're almost in firing range!" Marta called.

A second later the turbolift doors opened and Tuvok and Sozoas entered the bridge. Sozoas still held the black box.

"Friend Janeway," Sozoas said, "I must speak with the other ship. It is imperative."

"Of course," she said. "If there's anything you can do to defuse this situation, I'm in favor of it." She gave a quick nod to Harry Kim.

"Hailing frequencies open," Harry said.

Sozoas stepped forward and addressed the other ship in his whistley language. A moment later, another Sperian appeared on the monitor to answer. First Sozoas, then the other Sperian bowed ritually.

"They are decelerating and powering down weapons systems," Ensign Dvorak said softly.

"Keep monitoring them," Janeway said. She pulled Chakotay and Tuvok aside. "Can you provide a running translation?" she asked Tuvok.

"They are speaking a little quickly," he said, "but I will attempt it."

He listened for a moment, then began:

"I am Sozoas, subLeader for the Tech Faction's warp-acceleration-tube project. Identify yourself."

"I am Sezau, Leader of this Action Group."

"The Military Faction is dishonorable, treacherous, and inefficient," Sozoas said. "Your motives are based on greed and acted upon without skill."

Tuvok added, "This would appear to be an insult, but is a standard part of formally registering complaints between Factions."

Chakotay shook his head. "Neelix was right."

"I never would have guessed this exchange was mere ritual," Janeway said. "They're bickering like Ferengi." The more she learned of the Sperians, the less she liked them, she thought. More and more she suspected that the only thing which made Sozoas tolerable was his exposure to Tuvok's orderly, rational mind. She hadn't liked the effects Sozoas's mind had had on Tuvok nearly as much.

Sezau replied: "The Tech Faction's actions have incited us to movement. As always, Tech movements in Military Faction areas lie at the root of all interFaction conflict."

"Military Faction aggressive behavior—"

Tuvok broke off. "Do you want me to continue, Captain? Their dialog will continue along these lines for the immediate future."

Janeway nodded slowly; at least she had some time to figure out what to do. "About how long will this argument last?" she asked.

"It can go on for hours or even days in rare instances. It usually ends when one participant collapses from exhaustion, concedes the point, superiors intervene, or one side takes arbitrary decisive action."

"Which is most likely?" she asked.

"In this instance, I suspect arbitrary decisive action."

"An attack?" Chakotay asked.

"Precisely."

Janeway took a slow breath. "What about the other three ships?" Perhaps they could provide help against the Military Faction ship.

Chakotay said, "One of them has restored warp power already. Another will have it within twenty minutes. The third now anticipates finishing repairs in a little over an hour."

She nodded; better than she'd hoped. "Together," she said, "our four ships should be more than a match for this one. Only I'm not convinced the Sperians would come to our aid."

"Why not?" Chakotay demanded. "Do they want to die?"

"I am inclined to agree with the captain's assessment," Tuvok said. "The Sperians do not move rapidly, even to deal with crises such as this one. They are more likely to watch us be destroyed, then argue with the Military Faction's ship one by one until they, too, are destroyed."

"They wouldn't help us even if their own lives are at risk?" Chakotay said. "I find that hard to believe."

"Believe it," Janeway said. It certainly fit the pattern of behavior their culture had displayed so far, she thought.

"The situation is not hopeless," Tuvok went on. "The Sperians, I must point out, are no more suicidal than we are. Faced with a situation they cannot hope to win, I believe the Military Faction would eventually back down. We do outgun them at the moment, after all."

"Explain," Janeway said quickly.

"I refer to the warp-acceleration tube. B'Elanna should have finished slaving the controls to *Voyager* by now."

"That's right," Chakotay said. "We beamed her back aboard twenty minutes ago."

"Are you suggesting another near miss?" Janeway said. "How can we be sure the shock waves would knock out their ship and not ours? We won't get a second shot."

Tuvok raised an eyebrow. "I did not recommend a near miss. I suggested aiming the tube straight at them."

The idea was crazy, Janeway thought. Another product of the mind-meld? Certainly the old Tuvok would never have spoken of taking lives so casually. It went against everything in which they believed.

She said, "I can't blithely order the destruction of their ship—"

"I did not say to fire the tube," Tuvok said evenly, "merely to point it at them. Since they are responsible for turning it into a weapon, they must surely know its destructive capabilities."

"You're saying we should bluff," Chakotay said with a grin. "I thought Vulcans didn't bluff."

"Perhaps you have never played poker with a Vulcan," Tuvok said, regarding him. "I would welcome the chance to demonstrate at a more appropriate time."

"I may just take you up on that," Chakotay said.

It just might work, Janeway mused. The Military Faction could not possibly know they were bluffing.

"All right," she said, "we'll try it. How long will it take for the tube to power up as if to fire?"

"Two hours and twenty-seven minutes, according to the computer simulation we ran," Chakotay said.

"Get on it—but don't attract any attention. If we tip our hand, they may decide to attack now rather than talk us to death first."

"Aye, Captain." He strolled casually to the communications console and whispered a few commands to Harry Kim. Janeway realized they must have transferred the tube's controls to the communications station.

She watched Harry work for a few seconds, then glanced at Sozoas. She couldn't allow her attention to focus on Harry in case the Sperians noticed.

Sozoas actually seemed to be enjoying the argument, she thought. He stood with his feet planted firmly, his head back, and all his stems pointed straight at the monitor. The twittering flutter of his voice carried notes of rage and indignation.

The Sperian on the monitor matched him word for word and gesture for gesture; they were like two children bickering over a favorite toy. It was incredible, in a way. She never would have thought two sentient beings capable of such a display. Anywhere in the Alpha Quadrant, it would have been downright embarrassing.

Just a few hours more, she thought. *Keep it up, Sozoas. I'm counting on you and your damned argumentative nature.*

She hoped for once that Tuvok's rational and all too agreeable personality wouldn't suddenly show itself.

BREAKFAST HAD ALWAYS BEEN ONE OF HIS BEST MEALS.

Neelix looked down at the trays of steamed *phu*, lightly toasted Artelian sweetbreads, creamed Xantaxan mushrooms, and high-protein vegetable bars. Hardly any had been touched. Of the hundred-and-fifty-odd who normally showed up for breakfast, only twenty-two had made it in today. They sat singly or in pairs at the galley's tables, speaking in muted whispers and glancing around as if at a funeral. It made the room feel even more deserted than it actually was.

Paul Fairman had to be responsible, Neelix thought. He must have begun handing out breakfasts to the crew. *Replicated* breakfasts. Breakfasts with no soul or substance. And now the delicious meal he'd slaved over for an hour and a half would go to waste.

No, not waste, he thought. Their supplies had run too low for that. He'd add a few new sauces and reheat it for lunch. And if necessary, he'd reheat it again with fresh vegetables for dinner.

He touched his badge. "Neelix to Ensign Kim." This was the first breakfast Harry Kim had missed in weeks. He knew Harry would give him the answers he wanted.

"This isn't a good time, Neelix," Harry said.

"I just need the answer to one question," he said.

"Okay, but make it fast."

"Did Paul Fairman give you a replicated breakfast this morning?"

There was a long pause. Finally Harry said, "I'm sorry, but I promised I wouldn't answer that question. I've got to go. Kim out."

Neelix chewed his lip thoughtfully. Harry had promised not to answer that question? What did *that* mean? Fairman *must* have made Harry promise not to tell him.

But I gave him the power supply, Neelix thought. *I already know he has a replicator. Why wouldn't he want me to know he was serving breakfasts? Does he think I'm an idiot and can't figure it out for myself?*

If only Tuvok hadn't approved giving Fairman that power supply, none of this would have mattered. What had the Vulcan been thinking? What had he himself been thinking, for that matter? Replicators were nothing but trouble.

Then another thought came to him. Perhaps Fairman was trying to annoy him for some reason. Could this be some sort of weird human revenge? *I only made him stir a few pots for fifteen minutes,*

Neelix thought. The *phu* had boiled over, but that had been an accident. It could have happened to anyone. Why would Fairman resent him so much for it?

Perhaps it was a onetime thing, Neelix thought. Perhaps everyone would be back for lunch, like always. No sense in leaping to conclusions, after all.

But he had a strange unhappy feeling that things were only going to get worse.

B'Elanna stifled a yawn. She had been meaning to turn in and get some sleep, but fate seemed against her. Pulling a double shift aboard the warp-acceleration tube had left her exhausted, but the work just couldn't wait.

Lieutenant Carey was showing her the makeshift repairs on the warp core, and the diagnostics didn't look good. She knew what kind of abuse engines took in combat situations. These repairs had been done by the book, and under normal circumstances they'd hold out long enough for the ship to cruise to a nearby starbase for a complete overhaul. But they weren't cruising anywhere near a starbase, and if she knew Tom Paris, Chakotay, and the captain, they weren't going to be cruising anywhere. More like racing through an obstacle course.

"It's not going to hold," she said.

Carey nodded. "I thought it would do. The captain wanted the warp engines back on-line as soon as possible. We *have* warp capability."

"Not for long, and not above warp four. Get a crew back here on the double. I'll talk to the captain. If we can get another hour, we can get it stabilized at least."

"Aye, sir," he said with a frown. He turned and headed aft, calling names of crewmen.

B'Elanna sighed as she tapped her badge. The work never seemed to end. "Torres to Captain Janeway," she said.

"Janeway here," came the reply.

"Captain, we need to take the warp engines off-line."

"How long?"

"An hour, maybe an hour and a half."

"Are you aware of our situation?"

"Captain, we could have a major core breach if we don't realign the stabilizing grid. I wouldn't trust the ship above warp four without it."

The captain paused; B'Elanna knew she was weighing the pros and cons of the situation in her mind. At last she said, "Do it. Cut every second off your estimate that you can. Janeway out."

B'Elanna rolled up her sleeves. "Computer," she said, "prepare to take the warp core off-line."

Janeway spent the next hour watching the clock, watching Sozoas, and trying not to let her anxiety show. No warp capabilities and no weapons—if Sozoas didn't hold up his end of the argument, she'd really be up a creek without a paddle.

Slowly, trying not to intrude on the ongoing argument between the Sperians, she crossed the bridge to join Tuvok at the security station. Tuvok had been monitoring both B'Elanna's and Harry Kim's progress.

"How long till the warp accelerator is powered up?" she whispered.

"Twelve minutes, thirty-six seconds," Tuvok replied.

She tapped her badge. "Janeway to Torres," she said softly. "I need warp power in twelve minutes."

"You'll have it in ten, Captain," Torres replied.

"Thank you, Lieutenant." Perfect timing at last, she thought.

Then Sozoas took a step back. *"Bas sh'pa!"* he said. Then he turned his back on Sezau; all his stems pointed in other directions.

"He's wrapping it up," Tuvok said. "He's just signaled the end of the argument. It's Sezau's turn to act."

"What?" Janeway whirled in surprise. "We're not ready yet! Is there anything we can do to—"

Tuvok sprang forward, pushing Sozoas out of the way. The Vulcan planted his feet firmly, threw back his head, and declared: *"Na posh sza ksi Tuvok!"*

The Sperian captain regarded him silently for a second, then said, *"Za arsah Sezau, ksi zogu!"*

As Janeway watched, the bickering picked up right where it had left off, only this time between Tuvok and Sezau. But how long could the Vulcan keep it up? *Another ten minutes, that's all we need,* she thought. Hopefully he could make it last that long.

Janeway hurried forward, grabbed Sozoas by the arm, and pulled him to the side. "What did he say?" she demanded. "Why did you break off your dialog?"

"The Military Faction will not yield to reason. I could see no point in continuing the discussion. Logically, it has become a time for action."

"But Tuvok—"

The Sperian's stems bent toward the Vulcan. "For

some reason he has chosen to continue the discussion. However, Sezau is insulting him because he is an alien and not a true Faction participant. They are now debating whether Tuvok qualifies as a Faction Friend. Logically, Sezau will concede this point soon and they will move to more important matters."

"Thank you." Tuvok must have chosen an argument he could win to have the logical upper hand, she thought. He only had to spin it out for another six minutes . . . surely he could manage that.

She crossed to the communications station. "Status, Mr. Kim?" she asked.

"I have gradually brought the warp accelerator around. I don't believe they've noticed, but it's now pointing directly at them. The power buildup is nearly complete."

Janeway's badge chirped. "Torres to Janeway. Warp capability has been restored, Captain. I need two days to get it back up to specs, but as long as you keep us under warp seven we'll be fine."

"Acknowledged. Good job, B'Elanna." *We're going to make it,* she thought.

"Three minutes," Harry whispered.

Janeway turned to watch the argument continue. Both Tuvok and Sezau were gesturing animatedly. Tuvok seemed surprisingly emotional; was it the Sperian influence from the mind-meld or role-playing? She couldn't be sure.

"Two minutes," Harry said.

Janeway had once seen a Vulcan performance of *Hamlet.* Despite their personal lack of emotion, the Vulcans had managed to convey Shakespeare's emotional depth with surprising accuracy. They had studied human performances of the play and mimicked certain elements with a cool precision. That had to be what Tuvok was doing here . . . she hoped.

"One minute," Harry said.

"Mr. Paris," Janeway said.

"Yes, Captain," he said.

"Prepare to execute on my signal."

"The warp-acceleration tube is fully powered," Harry said.

"Now, Mr. Tuvok!" Janeway called.

"Mr. Paris," Janeway said, "are you still prepared to carry out evasive maneuvers?"

CHAPTER

21

TUVOK ABRUPTLY BROKE OFF HIS CONVERSATION, BOWED to Sezau, then spoke again in a quiet, frank manner. Janeway watched with interest. Would their plan work?

A second later Sezau jerked around and began calling orders to his crew. They scrambled to their stations.

"I have informed him," Tuvok said, "that we have powered up the warp-accelerator tube and now have the ability to destroy his ship. He is confirming this fact for himself."

Sezau turned and snarled something at Tuvok and Sozoas.

"He says we, like all aliens, are without honor or process and do not deserve his attention."

"Tell him he's right," Janeway said. According to Neelix, giving in was the best way to end an argument with a Sperian, after all.

Tuvok repeated her message.

"Tell him also that his ship is to remain where it is. Any movement will be considered a hostile act and met with appropriate force."

Again Tuvok translated.

"End the transmission," she said to Harry. "Open a secure link to the other three Sperian ships." Now she had to get everyone up and moving toward safety.

"Aye, Captain," Harry said. A second later he had the captain of the Tech Faction's lead ship on the monitor.

Janeway turned to Sozoas. "Tell him to leave this system immediately. As soon as they're safely away, we'll follow."

"I will instruct them to return to our home system," Sozoas said. "That is where I must present our case before the Council of Factions."

He spoke briefly with the other captain, who argued a few moments, then gave in. They ended the conversation. The viewscreen switched to an external view of the three ships. Kathryn felt a flood of relief when they began to accelerate, then they disappeared into warp. One less thing to worry about, she thought.

"The Military Faction ship is hailing us," Harry said.

"Put them on," Janeway said.

Sezau appeared on the viewscreen, speaking angrily. Sozoas replied, and they exchanged heated words for a few minutes. Slowly Janeway realized the argument had started again. This could take a while, she thought, so she returned to her chair and sat, crossing her legs comfortably. The longer they spun it out, the farther away the three Tech Faction ships would get.

Finally, some twenty minutes later, Sozoas turned to her and said, "He demanded to know where the other ships are going. I told him I ordered them back to our home base, and that they have taken evidence to present to the Council of Factions concerning the Military Faction's crimes in this system. There is now nothing he can do to cover up these events."

Sezau said something else, to which Sozoas began a lengthy reply.

Tuvok said, "Sezau has ordered us to surrender, and Sozoas in return has ordered him to surrender."

"Sever communications," Janeway said. "This is getting us nowhere." She turned to the Sperian. "Sozoas, if you will provide Mr. Paris with the coordinates, we will bring you home."

Sozoas bowed to Tom, then recited a short string of spatial references. "Speria, our homeworld, is only a day from here," he said to Janeway. "You will also be able to acquire any supplies you need. On behalf of the Tech Faction, I promise whatever assistance you need in appreciation for your help here."

"Thank you," Janeway said.

Tom said, "Course locked in."

"Please," Sozoas said, "one last favor. Before you leave, destroy the warp-accelerator tube."

"Why?" Janeway asked, surprised. That seemed a surprising move to her. "The Tech Faction has invested so much time and labor in it—and so many lives have already been lost over it—"

"Precisely," he said. "It is logical to assume that, if

we leave it behind, the Military Faction will claim it as salvage. Their only interest in it is as a weapon; they would continue research along those lines. I would not like to see it used for violence again."

"Captain," Tom said, "The other ship is accelerating away from us."

Janeway glanced up at the viewscreen just in time to see the Sperian ship disappear in a shimmer of rainbow colors. Had Sezau gone to warp speed in pursuit of the other three ships? Somehow, she didn't think so. He'd probably slunk home to report his failure . . . or argue about who was really to blame. But she had to be sure.

"Are they chasing the *A-Zha-Gor*, *A-Zir-Toin*, and *A-Zha-Tas*?" she asked.

"Negative," Tom said. "They set a different course."

"It was a situation they could not hope to win," Sozoas said. "Retreat seemed the most logical solution."

Janeway nodded. "I see your point." She tapped her badge. "Janeway to Torres."

B'Elanna answered at once: "Torres here."

"We can't leave the tube for the Military Faction to salvage. What's the best way to destroy it?"

"We can use its maneuvering thrusters to send it into the white dwarf," she suggested. "However, that's going to take some time."

"What if we give the tube a nudge with our tractor beam to get it up to speed?"

"That should do it."

"Thank you. Janeway out." She looked at Tom. "Coordinate your efforts with Ensign Dvorak," she said. Things seemed to be wrapping up quite nicely, she thought.

"Aye, Captain," Tom said with a grin. "Locking tractor beam on . . ."

Sozoas bowed. "On behalf of the Tech Faction, I thank you."

Janeway returned to her seat and leaned back. Harry had put a view of the warp-accelerator tube on the main viewscreen. She watched its thrusters fire, nudging it slowly toward the white dwarf. Then Tom locked on the tractor beam, giving it an added push. The tube began to move perceptibly faster.

Indeed, Janeway thought, it looked like things were working out better than she could have hoped. With the Tech Faction's support, they could see about some long-overdue maintenance to *Voyager*, not to mention fresh supplies and foodstuffs—and, of course, shore leave for the crew. Helping Sozoas might be the best thing that had happened to them in quite a while.

"Warp factor three, Mr. Paris," she said, crossing her arms. "On to Speria."

EPILOGUE

FROM THE OBSERVATION DECK OF THE SPERIAN SPACE station *Za Chii Lo*, which Tuvok had translated as *Step For All Factions*, Kathryn Janeway could see both the *Voyager* and the Sperians' home planet. *Voyager*, docked at the outermost ring alongside a half-dozen immense globe-shaped spaceships belonging to various Factions, displayed the same sleek, beautiful lines that had always impressed her so much. Beyond the space station, Speria—a lush blue-green M-class planet wisped with swirling white clouds—hung like a jewel in the darkness.

They had been docked here for a week now. It seemed like six months. *I can't wait to get back out into space*, she thought. She never wanted to meet another Sperian as long as she lived.

The various bickering Factions made every transaction an ordeal. Even with Tuvok translating and Sozoas trying to expedite matters, everything just dragged on and on and on. There was no pleasing them—and no agreeing with them. She had spent much of the last six days deadlocked in arguments with the Farmers Faction, who weren't getting along with the Tech Faction and were at present allied with the Military Faction. Twice she thought they'd concluded negotiations to lay in fresh food for Neelix, but each time new and barely relevant points had been raised by the Sperians.

It was almost as bad with the Industrial Faction. B'Elanna needed several new components for backup systems in the warp engines, but it didn't look like they'd get them anytime soon. It didn't look like they'd wind up with anything here but headaches.

At least the crew was enjoying shore leave. The Sperians might not have much to offer socially, but their planet had plenty of parks, and Neelix had organized a picnic for that afternoon. If she knew her morale officer, he'd have everyone dancing and laughing and enjoying a meal of chicken-fried *phu* or some such concoction.

She'd noticed an overall improvement in the crew's mood, though, so their time here hadn't been wasted. People were smiling and laughing again in the corridors. An almost palpable feeling of happiness filled the ship.

It was time to move on, though. Tomorrow they would leave, she decided, whether they had fresh supplies or not. She sighed. *Not* seemed far more likely.

* * *

The square dance was a delightful invention, Neelix reflected. He wished he'd thought of it himself. While *Voyager*'s crew clapped their hands and stomped their feet, the exuberant sounds of a bow fiddle filled the air. Tom Paris, acting as caller, ordered everyone to grab their partner and promenade.

Simply delightful, Neelix thought. They were going to be in high spirits when they got back to *Voyager* that night.

But now he was going to be late for his meeting. Slowly he backed away from the crowd, turned, and crossed to the bushes, where he'd stashed the little antigrav cart he'd borrowed from the Tech Faction. It was little more than a floating sled with push handles, but it moved small cargoes like his quite nicely. Pushing it before him, he headed for the conference center half a kilometer away. He'd arranged to meet Sozoas there, and he didn't want to be late.

Suddenly Kes came running. "I've been looking all over for you," she said. "I thought you might want to dance!"

"Normally I'd love to, dearest," Neelix said, glancing back toward the picnic, "but unfortunately I have business to attend to."

"What sort of business?"

"The captain hasn't been able to get supplies, so . . ." He shrugged modestly. It had been the least he could do to help out.

"So you're going to get them for her." Kes gave him a quick hug and a kiss. "That's why I love you, Neelix. You're always thinking of others. I know how you hate dealing with Sperians, and you're doing it anyway."

Neelix felt himself blush. "Well, yes, I am, aren't I?"

"Do you need any help?"

"No, I want you to stay here and have fun. I should be back soon."

"All right. But hurry!"

"I will, dearest!"

Kes headed back toward the picnic, and Neelix felt his heart quicken at the sight. She was so beautiful. He loved her more than anything in the universe.

But right now he had work to do, he reminded himself, so he began to push the antigrav cart down the curving flagstone path. Soon he reached the edge of the park. Opposite him, across a red brick highway over which buzzed any number of small silver sphere-shaped vehicles, stood the domed conference building where his meeting was scheduled to take place.

Sozoas had been waiting outside, on the broad red steps. Neelix spotted him and waved, then pushed the antigrav cart over.

"Did you bring it?" the Sperian asked as he approached.

"Right here!" Neelix patted the antigrav cart's handle.

"This way."

Sozoas opened the building wide door and Neelix maneuvered the cart inside. Natural light came in through narrow slits in the walls. The floor had been carpeted, and the walls had a smooth texture. It seemed much like every other Sperian building he'd ever been inside, Neelix thought.

They took a ramp to an upper level, where a round table with six chairs had been set up. Four Sperians already sat there. Sozoas joined them and seated himself in one of the empty chairs; Neelix took the other. Now, he thought, to get down to business.

"I have explained your proposal," Sozoas said to Neelix. "It seems only logical that we conclude this deal with all due haste, since your captain plans to leave in twelve of your hours."

"So soon?" Neelix said, frowning. He wasn't sure the deal could be concluded so quickly; he'd never heard of Sperians finishing anything in less than a week, and he'd considered himself lucky the last time he'd dealt with them to get away after only two weeks.

"I realize it does not leave us with much time, so let us come right to the point. We want what you are offering."

"I knew you would." Neelix removed the sheet covering the antigrav cart, revealing a bright red Reflux 2000 replicator. "Once you copy its design, it will be the solution to all your problems with the Farmers Faction: you will be able to create your own food from any energy source."

"We would like to see a demonstration."

"Certainly." Neelix cleared his throat, switched on the little replicator, and said, "Steamed *phu* in paguay sauce over blue noodles." He'd programmed the replicator for some of his own favorite recipes since borrowing it from Paul Fairman's cabin.

Seconds later a steaming plate appeared inside. Neelix lifted it out and set it on the table.

All the Sperians leaned forward, stems stretched out to their fullest. Several spoke. Sozoas replied, then handed out what looked like thimbles with two prongs attached, which Neelix recognized as eating implements. As he watched, the Sperians slipped thimbles onto the fingers of their left hands, then used the prongs to pick up pieces of *phu* and sample the delicacy.

As they ate, they began to argue among themselves.

"They can't decide if it has too much spice," Sozoas said. "Two believe it has too little, and one believes it's fine the way it is."

"Tell them the replicator can be programmed to individual tastes."

"I believe that would only give them further cause for discussion," Sozoas said.

"You know best," Neelix said with a shrug. He didn't really care, just so he got what he wanted. Reaching into his pocket, he pulled out a datachip. "This is a list of what I require in exchange for the replicator."

Sozoas accepted the datachip and plugged it into a slot in the table. "One ton of *paga*-root," he said. "One half ton of gelled *égrap*. Thirty kilograms of assorted Ortegan spice-blend. Thirty-six cubic meters of durasteel plating . . ." He read down the list, naming everything correctly.

When he finished, Neelix nodded. "All of that to be delivered to *Voyager* before our departure in twelve hours."

"Are there any other terms?"

"Simply that this replicator is to be considered proprietary technology. You may use it only within your own race. It is not to be shared with anyone else . . . neither traded nor given away."

"I believe," Sozoas said, "that it will only be used

within the Tech Faction. I can see no reason to share it with any other Faction."

"Then we're in agreement."

Sozoas spoke quickly with the other four. At times they argued, but each time Sozoas seemed prepared: he must have thought it all out and had his arguments ready, Neelix thought. It was exactly what Tuvok would have done in the same situation.

Half an hour later, Sozoas turned to him and bowed. "It is agreed," he said simply. "The materials will be delivered to *Voyager* shortly."

Neelix smiled and bowed. "I do, however, need the power supply back from the replicator," he said. "It's not mine to give away."

"Take it," Sozoas said.

Neelix reached forward, unclipped the power supply, and stuck it into his largest front pocket. Then he smiled. Everything had worked out exactly as he'd hoped.

Twelve hours later, Kathryn Janeway stood on the bridge watching the Sperian space station slowly dwindle behind them on the viewscreen. It shrank to a mere pinprick, then vanished altogether. It hadn't happened too soon for her, she thought.

"Warp four, Mr. Paris," she said. "Resume our course for home."

"Aye, Captain," he said. "Coming about on our old heading."

"I'll be in my ready room," she said. "Chakotay, you have the bridge."

She went in and sat at her desk. Fourteen new reports to read, she thought with an inward groan.

You'd think that with a week of shore leave no paperwork would have been finished. Half the crew had elected to work aboard the ship to get things back to normal, skipping part of their leave. That was dedication, she thought.

She began paging through the reports. The first was from B'Elanna, giving a list of engineering problems and the materials needed to fix them. Janeway flipped past it; she'd come back to that one later, since she knew it would depress her.

A report from Neelix caught her eye. It was a list of materials he had acquired on Speria, she realized, which were currently stored in docking bays two and three. She gave a low whistle as she looked it over. Tons of food . . . durasteel plating . . . warp-core insular thermocouplings . . . was there anything he'd missed?

She flipped back to B'Elanna's report. Except for the foodstuffs, the two lists were identical. Somehow Neelix had managed to get everything B'Elanna needed. But how? She'd tried for a week with no success.

She tapped her badge. "Janeway to Neelix."

"Neelix here," he replied. "I take it you've seen my report, Captain?"

"Yes . . . but how did you manage to acquire all these materials?"

Neelix chuckled. "Secret of the trade, my dear captain. Will you be down for breakfast soon? I have something new—sponge cakes topped with finely ground Sperian treenuts."

"That sounds delicious," Janeway said. She hadn't had a sponge cake in years.

"Believe me, it is," Neelix said. "I was fortunate enough to get a hundred freshwater Sperian sponges, and they cooked up deliciously!"

"Freshwater sponges?" she asked doubtfully.

"The flavor *is* a little more delicate than the saltwater sponges of Helorius Seven, but I think you'll find the lighter texture is worth it. Now—"

"Yes, well, carry on," Janeway said. She swallowed; her appetite seemed to have suddenly vanished. "I'll be down as soon as I finish up this paperwork."

"I'll save you an extra-large slice!" he promised.

Paul Fairman awakened slowly, luxuriating in the newfound power that was his to command. They were under way now, he thought, so it was time to get back to business. He hadn't used his replicator during their stopover on the Sperian space station; there were too many native delicacies for the crew to try. Now that they were back in space, however, it was a different story. He knew everyone would be pining for home-cooked meals.

He'd used his first set of favors to make sure everyone would keep quiet about the replicator. The second set, though . . . now was when he'd really start to collect. He wouldn't work another shift for the rest of the voyage.

Rubbing his hands, he opened the closet to pull out his private replicator—but it was empty. No, he took that back. The power supply was still there; only the replicator itself was gone. He stared at the empty space where he'd last seen his Reflux 2000, shocked. All his plans. All his private deals. Who could have stolen it?

"Computer," he said. "Besides me, how many people have been in this cabin in the last twenty-four hours?"

"One other person has been in this cabin," the computer said.

"Who was it?" he asked.

"Morale Officer Neelix."

"What!" he cried. Fairman felt a cold rage surge through him. It figured that sawed-off scavenger would steal his replicator. It was probably in the galley now, spitting out *phu*-loaf for everyone aboard ship. Well, he wasn't going to put up with it. A deal was a deal, and he'd make Neelix live up to his end if he had to choke his scrawny little neck to do it!

He stomped out of his cabin and down to the galley. Luckily breakfast had just begun; there were only a couple of Starfleet crewmen there, and they seemed too wrapped up in their discussion to pay any attention to him.

Neelix stood among the pots and pans, mashing a pale blue root of some kind with a wooden mallet. Grinding his teeth in rage, Fairman stalked over. He'd ring the alien's neck, all right, he thought.

Neelix merely grinned and set down his mallet. "Welcome, Paul Fairman!" he said, giving him a quick hug. "What brings you down here so early? How about a sponge cake? Or the braised *taba*-root will be ready in about ten minutes—"

"You know why I'm here," Fairman said, letting a dangerous edge creep into his voice. "You took my replicator."

"You know," Neelix said, putting an arm around Fairman's shoulders—which Paul promptly removed. "When I agreed to provide you with a power supply," you said I could have anything I wanted in trade. It took me a while to find what you had that I needed, but it turned out to be that replicator."

"The whole point of getting the power supply," Fairman hissed, "was to run the replicator. Without the replicator, I have no need for the power supply!"

"That does make a certain amount of sense," Neelix admitted, "and I'm sorry if my taking it caused you any inconvenience, but—"

"Just—give—it—back!" Fairman said. He didn't think he could make it any more clear than that.

"There *is* a problem," Neelix said.

Fairman felt himself slipping toward losing control. He fought to hold back his anger.

"What sort of problem?" he managed to say.

"You see, you were on station leave when I needed it, so I couldn't ask—"

"Get to the point!"

"In short," Neelix said, "I traded it to the Tech Faction for food supplies for the galley, seedlings for the hydroponics garden, and all the necessary parts to repair the warp engines and the hull breaches—"

"No," Fairman groaned. His knees felt weak. Suddenly he had to sit down. He sank onto a three-legged wooden stool that Neelix had somehow procured for the galley.

"Why, the sponges for the sponge cake were only *one* of the delicacies I've acquired," Neelix went on, all but bubbling with enthusiasm, "and your replicator could never have matched their texture. And we got spores to grow our own in the hydroponics garden!"

"Wonderful," Fairman said bitterly. "I'll be looking forward to it." He rose a little unsteadily. "Now, if you'll excuse me, I think I'm going to be ill."

"In that case," Neelix called after him, "I'll stop by your cabin a little later to cheer you up. A little singing is what you need, and I'm just the fellow to do it! Paul? *Paul?*"

Back on the bridge, Kathryn Janeway stood looking out at the stars. Somewhere out there, she thought, there has to be a shortcut home. The Sperians' warp-acceleration project had only encouraged that hope. There were other sentient beings here looking for ways to travel farther, faster than they'd ever gone before. One of them had to have succeeded.

Seventy thousand light-years to Earth. They'd made it this far. They could make it home again. She closed her eyes and thought, for a second, of everyone and everything she'd left behind.

I promise you, she thought, *I'll be home soon.*